13.95

A

M/

TOBY THE SPLENDID

For all my animals

TOBY THE SPLENDID

also by
Isabelle Holland

Henry and Grudge

A Horse Named Peaceable

Now Is Not Too Late

Dinah and the Green Fat Kingdom

Alan and the Animal Kingdom

TOBY THE SPLENDID

Isabelle Holland

WALKER AND COMPANY
NEW YORK

Text copyright © 1987 Isabelle Holland

First published in the United States of America in 1987 by the

Walker Publishing Company, Inc.

Published simultaneously in Canada by John Wiley & Sons

Canada, Limited, Rexdale, Ontario.

Library of Congress Cataloging-in-Publication Data

Book design by Catherine Gallagher

Library of Congress Cataloging-in-Publication Data

Holland, Isabelle.
   Toby the splendid.

   Summary: After going against her mother's wishes
and buying a horse with her baby sitting money,
thirteen-year-old Janet works for his upkeep in
the stables but finds she has no extra money for
the riding lessons she desperately wants.
   [1. Horses—Fiction. 2. Mothers and daughters—
Fiction] I. Title.
PZ7.H7083To   1987   [Fic]   86-24681
ISBN 0-8027-6674-9

Printed in the United States of America

10 9 8 7 6 5 4 3 2 1

CHAPTER 1

I've wanted a horse ever since I can remember. But from the first moment I mentioned it to Mother—just after my thirteenth birthday a year ago—she was against it.

"It's dangerous and expensive," she said. "There are lots of better and healthier things you can do, and I'll help you out with any of them. But not riding."

"Kids I know at school ride, and they're no richer than us."

"People who ride sooner or later want to show horses or hunt, and they are both outlandishly expensive hobbies. We can't afford that, Janet, and I don't want you to get mixed up with that lot."

"I don't see that it's that dangerous. Sure, people get hurt sometimes, but they get hurt playing sports or on bicycles, and—"

Mother didn't even let me finish. "Angela Blair, in my office, will be on crutches for the rest of her life because a horse fell on her. The answer, Janet, is no. Definitely no. I will not buy you a horse for your birthday or Christmas. End of subject."

I didn't ask Mother for a horse again. I started babysitting instead. When Mother asked me why, I said, as vaguely as I could, that I wanted pocket money and anyway (going on the offensive), why did she mind since she always told us how she babysat to help get through college? Since Mother has always been a great believer in the work ethic, she let it go at that.

A year later, a week after my fourteenth birthday, I answered an ad in our local paper and bought Toby for four hundred dollars. I'd already made arrangements with Smith Farm, which was near enough for me to reach on my bicycle. So I had Toby delivered there before telling Mother anything.

When I did, she was furious. "You know I would have forbidden you to do this!" she said.

I did indeed know, or at least guessed, which was why I hadn't said anything about it. "Since it won't interfere with school I don't see why you mind. I'm not asking you to pay for Toby."

"It's not just paying for the horse, for heaven's sake, Janet! It's the upkeep, the stabling, the food, the riding clothes and lessons, the vet bill if the wretched animal falls sick. Buying the horse is only the beginning."

I had begun to appreciate how true that was the moment Toby arrived at Smith barn and started eating. It wasn't that Mrs. Smith hadn't been up front with exactly how much Toby's upkeep would cost. It was more that I was so taken up with finding him, buying him and getting him there that I hadn't thought too clearly beyond that. And I could see now, as Mother laid down the law, that I had secretly been hoping that, once faced with the fact that I had bought the horse, Mother would help in its running expense. Obviously she wasn't going to. Keeping Toby in feed and shelter was going to mean a lot of babysitting and mucking out.

We were in the kitchen getting ready for dinner when we had that conversation. As we talked, I caught

2

sight of my sister, Cynthia, crossing the yard on her way in. "You didn't mind when Cynthia thought she wanted to be a ballet dancer and went to class four nights a week. And you paid for that."

There was a silence. Finally Mother said, "That's not a fair comparison. Ballet is not dangerous, nor does it have an increasing scale of expense. I was glad for Cynthia to do it. I'm not at all glad over what you've done. How you're going to pay for the horse's upkeep I don't know. But that is now your problem. If your schoolwork suffers at all then you'll have to get rid of him."

At least she hadn't told me that no matter what I had to get rid of Toby. But the threat was there, waiting for the moment a grade went down or anything else in my life went the slightest bit wrong. The relationship between Mother and me, which had never been really good, changed for the worse: I knew that from now on I would have to think of everything I said and did in terms of how it might affect Toby.

"Buying that horse was really dumb," Cynthia said when dinner was over and we were going upstairs. "You knew how Mother feels about the whole riding bit."

"It's not dumb because I wanted a horse more than anything. With you it's different. Mom approves of everything you do. She never has with me."

"That's not true, Jan. And when you do want to do something she doesn't like, you go about it the wrong way."

"What's the right way?"

"You could have talked to her. She can see reason. You could've worked it out ahead of time and proved it could be done practically instead of buying first and telling her afterwards. At least she would have felt that she had some say in the matter."

"Her say would have been no."

"I don't think that's necessarily true. Now you make her think you don't care how she feels."

"She doesn't care how I feel."

"If you don't tell her, how can she care?"

"If I do tell her, she says no first."

It was back to square one, which is often where discussions between Cynthia and me get stuck.

Cynthia is sixteen and looks the way Mom must have looked at her age: tall and slim with dark hair and eyes. People say she's the prettiest girl in school, and they're probably right.

Once, when I'd overheard Mother talk about Cynthia on the phone, I made up some doggerel, using all the adjectives she had:

> *Sensitive, vulnerable, thin,*
> *Perceptive and certain to win,*
> *Slim and beautiful,*
> *Tall, immutable (I looked that up;*
>   *it means unchangeable.)*
> *That's the history of Cyn.*

I'm much smaller, with straw-colored hair and gray eyes, and I'm not pretty. People at school sometimes look at me and say in a surprised voice, "You're Cynthia West's sister, aren't you?"

"Yes," I said, knowing what's coming.

"You certainly don't look like her."

"No, I don't."

"Your mother's a lawyer, isn't she?"

"Yes."

"That's great. Do you plan to be a lawyer?"

"No."

"Well, I guess you have to be pretty bright for that."

4

"Yes."

I'm the me that is, I'd think to myself. The me that's not like Cynthia or like Mom, not the nonperson other people sometimes make me feel.

So I made up another rhyme.

> *Janet the nerd the herd the bird.*
> *Janet the bumbler and bumpkin*
> *Janet the bump*
> *The incredible lump—*

Once I asked Mom if I looked like Father. He died when I was four and I have no memory of him at all. Cynthia, of course, remembers him.

"Not really," Mom said. She put her head on one side. "Maybe a little."

That night I went and stared at his picture. If there was any resemblance I didn't see it. But Mom once said that he was quiet and didn't talk easily with people, and I certainly knew that I'd inherited that. Somehow I'd never been able to make friends at school the way Cynthia had. Cynthia and all the kids I knew had best friends. The nearest person to being my best friend was Morris Blair, who sat next to me in English class. But he was a boy, so he didn't really count.

After I got Toby it was all right. He became my best friend, we communicated perfectly, and I loved him more than anything in the world.

Toby is not beautiful. He's not very big and his knees are inclined to stick out. Also some Arabian ancestor had bequeathed him his short head and slightly dish face. But he has a beautiful soul and is a wonderful ride, and grooming him is the best therapy for anything that ails me.

One afternoon, a few months after I got him, as I

5

combed and brushed his coat, I talked to the dappled gray horse and told him my troubles.

"You're the top, Toby," I said. "The absolute A-one. You don't think I'm a nonperson, do you?"

Obligingly, Toby whinnied.

"Thank you."

Mrs. Smith, who owns the stable, came in at that moment and went to Aldebaran's stall. I was glad I'd cleaned it out when I first came in. Aldebaran is her mare and is part Thoroughbred, and Mrs. Smith is schooling her for the horse shows in the spring.

"Hello, Janet. Nice to see you. How's Toby?"

"He's fine." And then something popped out of my head that I hadn't planned and didn't even know I had thought about. "Do you think if I work this year and next spring with Toby I could compete in one of the horse shows the following summer? I mean the bottom class, of course."

Mrs. Smith, who is kind, but rather reserved, stopped brushing Aldebaran for a moment and looked at me. Then she said, "How much schooling have you had?"

"Just what I've had here."

Mrs. Smith herself had never coached me. For one thing, I couldn't afford the lessons. But every now and then, if I had finished my chores, Betsy, the chief barn girl, would take me out to the ring and give me a few pointers. I had learned, more or less, how to hold the reins, how to try to achieve a good seat and not bounce around too much, how to rise on every other trot, plus a whole category of things not to do.

"What you really need," Betsy had said the last time in the ring, "is some intensive coaching. Right now you look like a sack of potatoes in the saddle." My face must have collapsed, because she added kindly, "Everybody

6

does at first. All you need is some decent schooling. You have a good relationship with your horse, which is the most important thing of all, and that means you are a considerate rider. I wouldn't give you a penny for the best rider in the horse show if all he's thinking about is how well he looks and not about his horse."

That cheered me up, but her reference to a sack of potatoes loomed large in my mind as Mrs. Smith looked at me.

"I guess Betsy fitted you in between lessons."

I nodded. She probably guessed that I couldn't have afforded to take proper lessons and knew my work in the stable—plus babysitting, of course—covered only Toby's upkeep.

"Lessons are normally fifty dollars an hour. I suppose you know that."

My heart sank. "Yes." I could never afford that. And there was no use even thinking of Mother. Suddenly there slid into my mind the three weeks the previous summer that Cynthia had spent with a friend who'd moved to California. The air fare alone would have paid for a half dozen riding lessons, and I hadn't gone anywhere during the summer except for the week all three of us had had on the Cape. Could I present riding lessons to Mother as a sort of balance to what Cynthia had had the previous year?

The answer to that was easy: No.

What burned me up was that if I were to take a summer school course in math or incur some other expenses to do with the school, Mother would produce the money in an instant. But not for Toby. I was already up to my ears in babysitting and mucking out. There wasn't one half hour left in my week that I could give to earning more money. No matter how hard I tried or how many hours I worked, I didn't have the money for riding lessons. Mother's angry words filled my head: "It's not just the price of the horse, it's the upkeep, the stabling, the riding clothes and lessons . . . But that's your problem."

She was right, I thought bitterly, it was.

I glanced up to see Mrs. Smith watching me, and blurted out, "Betsy said I looked like a sack of potatoes on a horse. Anyway," I went on, "I don't have any money for lessons." I started putting a saddle on Toby.

"Going out now?" Mrs. Smith asked.

"Yes."

"Well, I'll go out with you. We can go along the maple trail and I'll see whether I agree with Betsy or not. Then we can talk."

"Thanks," I said, surprised.

The maple trail was a pretty route that went through the Smiths' property and into a state park where there were plenty of bridle paths. There it followed a stream for a mile or two, then veered up and over one of the hills. Coming back another way, it turned into a broad, tree-lined avenue long enough for a horse to gallop, and that led back to the Smiths' farm. It was about an hour and a half ride and was a good one for anyone who wanted to try out a horse's gaits—walk, trot, canter and gallop.

Aldebaran is a tall, neatly shaped bay with clean lines and a look of breeding. Beside her, Toby was a real proletarian, but it didn't matter. Toby was Toby and I wouldn't have swapped him for Secretariat.

We rode mostly in silence, though Mrs. Smith would occasionally make a suggestion that was easier to follow and more helpful than Betsy's confrontational manner.

When we walked our horses up the hill, the view at the top was magnificent. Below us, at the bottom of the long sloping hill, was a lake, and we rested the horses and watched the sailboats and dinghies for a while. There were even a few swimmers, though the water at this point in late April was extremely cold. Then we walked the horses down and back over the hill and trotted towards the broad maple avenue.

"Okay, now canter!" Mrs. Smith said. "I'll sit here and watch for a moment and then follow. When I yell 'gallop!' I want you to gallop and bring Toby to a slow finish at the end of the avenue. All right now. Off you go!"

I gave Toby a little pressure from my legs and he responded, stepping out into a brisk trot. Then I gave him more leg and he broke willingly and enthusiastically into a canter. Toby's trot was a little jumpy, but his canter was the nearest thing I knew to flying in a rocking chair.

The trees flew past. I pushed my jumping cap back off my head a little and resisted the temptation to take it off altogether and let it hang by its strap. I didn't think Mrs. Smith would approve of that. The air rushed past my face. I could feel Toby's sturdy body beneath me and it was as though he and I were responding to one impulse of heart and muscle. It was moments like this that I wish I could describe properly to Mother. She'd understand then, and I wouldn't be afraid every time I saw her that she was about to tell me that I had to get rid of Toby.

"Gallop!" Mrs. Smith's voice yelled from behind.

"All right, Toby. Let's go," I said. "Let her see what a terrific galloper you are!" I gave him more leg, and he leaped beneath me. The trees were now a green blur, the grass between a dark-green. I tried to keep my eyes on the path to make sure that Toby didn't stumble on a rock or into a hole. With the best care in the world,

9

it was impossible to keep a path free of every possible hazard.

"Slow down now, gently and easily."

I pulled on the reins, trying to keep my hands steady so that the bit wouldn't hurt Toby's mouth. Finally, we stopped.

Mrs. Smith came trotting up behind. "You have a nice horse there, and you both like cantering and galloping. You work well together, but Betsy is right about your seat and one or two other things. Let's walk now."

We walked the horses for a few minutes, Aldebaran with his rider towering over Toby and me.

"How often are you coming to the stable now? Every day? I suppose you must, to exercise Toby, because I don't think you have an exercise agreement with us. Do you?"

"No. I come every day to exercise him, and I muck out after that and also Saturday and Sunday."

"And you do this along with school and homework, of course."

"Yes."

"You're Jane West's daughter, aren't you?"

"Yes." Somehow I knew the question that was coming. It came.

"How does your mother feel about your working here?"

Suddenly in my mind I saw Mrs. Smith deciding I couldn't use her farm because Mother disapproved of it, either because Mrs. Smith had strong views about parental permission or because she was one of Mother's many admirers. And then I saw Toby being led out to auction. So I lied.

"Mother likes us to have outside interests." It was half a lie. Mother did like us to have outside interests—but not Toby. "I don't suppose," I said, "that you have

any need for a babysitter? I do quite a lot of that, too."
What I would do about the Turners if she said yes I
didn't know, but I decided I'd worry about that later.

"No. But there's something else that might work
out. Do you do any coaching? My daughter, Mia, could
use some help with the exams she's going to have to
pass. She's not a student and she doesn't like study. On
the other hand, she wants to get into a boarding school
next year, and she's not going to make it if her grades
don't get better."

"Math?" I asked, devoutly hoping it wasn't.

"No, mostly English and French. You'd think she
never had a grammar lesson in her life. It's disheartening, to say the least. When she tries to write, she sounds
like an illiterate. If you could get her to the point where
she could pass that wretched test, I'd be unendingly
grateful—and I'd be glad to give you a couple of lessons
a week. How about it?"

When I was going to fit it in, I didn't know. But
that didn't matter. I'd do it somehow. And it was so
much more than I had hoped for that I was speechless
for a moment. Then I stammered out, "That's wonderful! I can't thank you enough! Will you tell me when it'll
be convenient?"

"Certainly. I'll confer with her and call you. That's
fine then, and I think you should join the Pony Club.
We can talk about that later, but it'll give you and Toby
outings with other kids your age. They're a lot of fun,
and you learn a lot about riding and taking care of your
horse. Now let's trot back or I'll be late for my next
coaching."

CHAPTER 2

Nothing happened for a few days. I didn't hear from Mrs. Smith and tried not to feel too disappointed. And then one day when I got home there was a large manila envelope addressed to me, with the return address, "Pony Club," in one corner. I took it quickly before Mother could get home, but I wasn't quick enough. Mother had come home earlier than usual and had seen the envelope lying on the hall table. At dinner she said suddenly, "What's the Pony Club?"

"It's a club for kids who ride. They have meetings and rallies and play games and do trail rides. It's a good way to learn how to ride along with a bunch of other kids."

Mother didn't say anything for a moment, then she asked, "How much does it cost?"

"Thirty dollars a year." If I'd left it at that, everything might have been all right. But I was so scared that she'd say it was one more thing that would interfere with school I blurted out, "I heard Betsy say it's the kind of thing that brings in the whole family."

It was the worst thing I could have said. In my anxiety I had forgotten that this was the year Mother was hoping to become a partner in her law firm and was

12

working harder than ever on a case involving a take-over by a client. Once she had said that if this case went well, she was almost certain to be offered a partnership.

"How?" she asked now. "By my being a sort of den mother to a pack of children on ponies, bringing the soda and sandwiches and standing around in the sun deciding who rides better than whom—like all the suburban mothers who have nothing better to do?"

"You don't have to," I said quickly. "It's not for mothers who have jobs—careers."

"And as for the money—"

"I'll pay it. I have some money saved." It was a lie. I'd just spent the last of my baby-sitting money for some boots—a major item. But I'd scrounge the money somehow.

"I'll lend you some," Cynthia said.

I couldn't have been more astonished. "Thanks," I said. "That's great!"

"As I've said before, it's not just the money." Mother began to gather our dishes to put in the dishwasher. "I hate to see you so obsessed with this whole thing. You're never home immediately after school. You're always rushing off either to that wretched stable or to babysit so you can keep your horse in hay or whatever it eats. I'd like to see you make more friends at school, maybe bring them home."

I could feel the old trap closing around me again. I never could make friends the way Cynthia could. Before Toby I'd just come home alone and pretend that it didn't matter. Remembering this so clearly, I should have kept my mouth shut. I should have stuck to my own first rule: Where Toby is concerned, flight is better than fight. But panic pushed the words out of my mouth.

"If I was home I'd be here alone. You're not here, and Cynthia is pretty busy after school, too, with her drama and ballet classes and hanging out at the soda shop."

"That's different," Mother started. Then she stopped. She put the last dishes in the dishwasher, then began slicing some fruit for dessert.

I didn't dare open my mouth. So it was Cynthia who said, "How different?"

Mother looked up from cutting the fruit, obviously surprised.

"Cynthia . . ." I said, hating myself for being such a coward. But being a coward was better than seeing Toby go off to an auction.

"I mean," Cynthia said calmly, "that Janet works terribly hard to pay for Toby and never asks you for a penny extra because she's scared you'll use it as an excuse not to let her ride. But you don't tell me I'll have to leave the drama club if I don't toe the line."

"I'm delighted you're in the drama club. You learn a lot from that. But what in God's name can Janet learn at that wretched stable except how to stay dirty most of the time—I can smell horse and stable every time I go into her bedroom—and how to learn a hobby that'll be no earthly use to her. Riding isn't a career. It doesn't take an ounce of brains. It's favored by snobs who hobnob with other snobs."

"Mom," Cynthia said, "you're being unfair."

Mother paused. "Am I? It doesn't feel that way to me. I just don't want Janet to spend all her time doing things like cleaning out stables when she could be making some of the more interesting clubs at school, not to mention working towards some kind of career. It's not too soon for that. Didn't the physics teacher take the science club on a tour of the local NASA place?"

"Yes," Cynthia said. "He did. I couldn't go because of the play. But if you're not interested in the science

14

club, Mom, then it's no great thing to go. Like I said, you're not being fair."

I stared down at my uneaten fruit. Tears pushed into my eyes, not because of Mother, but because of Cynthia. "Watch out," I said, "You'll push George out of the way." George is my imaginary friend and defender, named after St. George of dragon fame.

"Who's George?"

But I'd gone too far. I'd never place knowledge of my secret defender in anyone's hands, not even Cynthia's. "Just a friend," I said.

Suddenly Mother's hand clasped my shoulder. "I don't mean to be unfair, Jan. I want to do what's right for your own good. And it's not the money. I can give you the thirty dollars for your pony club—"

I jumped up, "Oh, Mom, that's terrific. It really is! And Toby is—"

"No, don't try to convert me to horses. It won't work." She smiled. "Your schoolwork had better not suffer, or no more Pony Club."

Later I went to Cynthia's room. She was, as usual, on the phone. Mother had an extra phone put into her room because she said she'd never be able to get any calls of her own if she didn't. I couldn't help wondering how much that extra phone cost as I stood in the door and waited for her to notice me.

She murmured something into the phone, then put it on her shoulder and said, "Yes?"

"Listen, I just wanted to say thanks."

Cynthia grinned. "You owe me one."

"Absolutely!"

"Good night," she said, still shouldering the phone.

"Good night."

If it had been a girl she was talking to, I reasoned, going up the stairs, she wouldn't have been so secretive.

Idly I wondered which boy it was: Alan Grant, Cynthia's great heartthrob and the one that most of the rest of the senior class was in love with?

The next morning I found an envelope stuck under the door. Inside was thirty dollars plus a note in Mother's handwriting. "Much love. Sorry to be such a pain in the neck. Have fun!"

CHAPTER 3

I gave the thirty dollars to Mrs. Smith that night, and she told me that she wanted me to coach Mia, her daughter, on Saturday mornings. Then she'd give me a coaching lesson right afterward, so that on the Saturdays the Pony Club met it still wouldn't interfere. And I'd have another lesson Wednesday evening.

The following Saturday I arrived at the stable at seven in the morning, cleaned out Toby's stall, helped Betsy for an hour, and then rang the bell at the Smith's farmhouse. Mrs. Smith opened the door.

"Mia's upstairs in her room," she said. "I guess it's only fair to warn you that her resistance to the idea of having a coach is total. Only the thought that it might get her into boarding school made her agree." She glanced at me, hesitated for a moment, then said, "Good luck!"

The Smiths' house was long and plain and rather elegant. It was made of a light gray stone and looked old. Somebody once told me that parts of it, including the framework, were pre-Revolutionary. Inside, the ceilings were low and whitewashed, and the furniture was made of some kind of dark wood and looked as old as the house.

I went up the stairs and turned right. The second door I came to was open. A girl of about my own age was sitting on a window seat staring out the window. She didn't turn when I came in, although she couldn't have avoided hearing me.

"Mia?" I said.

"Yeah. Who wants me?" She turned her head. Deep set eyes looked out from a thin, triangular face. Above were shaggy blond bangs.

"I'm Janet West," I said. "I'm supposed to . . . to coach you in French and English."

She didn't move. "Lotsa luck," she said.

"I thought you wanted to get into a boarding school."

"That what Ma told you?"

"Yes."

"Did she tell you what boarding school?"

"No."

"Well the one she's going to let me go to is one in Virginia. Everybody has a horse. Everybody rides. It'd be just like this place only worse."

"Where did you want to go to?"

"I wanted to go to Broadhurst's. Ever heard of it?"

I shook my head.

"Nobody in this lousy hole has. It's near New York, coeducational, has open classroom and specializes in drama. Naturally, Ma disapproves."

"Where do you go to school here?"

"Miss Mary's." It was said with a sneer. "All ladies. Lots of riding. Just like here."

"Don't you like riding?"

She'd turned her head away, but she looked back. "I loathe it. I hate—absolutely hate—horses. They're large, stupid beasts, pampered and overfed, and people who have them can't seem to talk about anything else."

18

I stared at her, then I started to laugh. I couldn't help it, even though I saw my coaching lessons disappearing down the hole.

"What's so funny?"

"Us. You and me and our mothers. Mine feels the way you do about horses. I spend my time not talking about Toby, my horse here, so she won't suddenly say I have to sell him. We ought to switch mothers."

"Any time! When do we start?"

I sat down at a table in the middle of the room and put my book satchel down on the floor. "So what do we do? I could try and coach you against your will, but it wouldn't work, would it?"

She grinned. "Not if I have anything to say about it."

There went my coaching. "I'll have to tell Mrs. Smith why I can't coach you."

"Go ahead! She knows anyway."

I sat there, computing how many more hours mucking out I'd have to do to pay for even one lesson. The answer to that was easy. Ten. And I was already committed to as much as I could manage. Ten hours would mean an extra hour for five days—that would add up to twenty-five dollars. Two extra hours for two days would bring it to forty-five dollars and I'd still be half an hour short. Maybe if I mucked out two extra hours for three days . . .

"What's Ma paying you for tutoring me?"

"She's paying me two riding lessons a week."

Mia shrugged. "So give her the money!"

The way she said it infuriated me. "It must be nice to be rich," I said nastily, getting up. I walked to the door. There was no way on earth I could make this girl study if she didn't want to, and I certainly wasn't going to grovel for her money.

"Hey! Just a minute. What did you mean by that crack about rich?"

I turned at the door. "Just what I said. A French queen once said more or less the same thing—'Let them eat cake!' "

"You mean you don't have the dough?"

"That's right."

She got up suddenly and went to a bookcase that lined the lower half of her wall. Pulling out a book, she opened it. A bundle of cash was stashed inside just the way I'd seen in spy movies.

"You in the CIA or something?"

"I don't know how much of a telltale you are, but I'd just as soon you wouldn't let on to Ma about where I keep some money."

"I'm not a telltale at all."

"You were going to tell her about why you couldn't coach me."

"What do you expect me to say? That I can't coach you because I'm too stupid? Why should I protect you? Because of you I won't get any coaching. But I'm not going to tell her you keep your money in a book, just like some grade-B movie."

She counted out some money and held it out. "Here's a hundred dollars. It'll buy you two lessons. Maybe Ma'll think you're so good she'll give you the rest for free. You'll show credit to her horse farm."

For a second I stared at the money.

Oddles and oodles of green megabucks
Bring coaching and riding the big megalucks . . .

*   *   *

"Come on," Mia said. "Take it. It won't bite!" I shook my head and walked out.

20

I told the whole thing to Toby as I brushed and groomed him before taking him out. "It stinks," I said. "Cynthia has a personal private telephone line but I can't have coaching lessons."

But a phone line didn't cost fifty dollars a week, let alone a hundred.

> *Ride a cock horse*
> *To Banbury Cross*
> *And see the adults*
> *On their tails take a toss . . .*

I was singing it to "Here we go round a mulberry bush," when I suddenly heard Mrs. Smith's voice.

"What is that you're singing?"

"Nothing," I said.

She appeared around the back of the stall, curry brush in hand. She must have been grooming Aldebaran, I thought, and glanced back. Aldebaran's stall was at the other end, so how Mrs. Smith heard me—and then I saw the mare was tethered with cross ties in the courtyard in the middle of the stable.

"Since you're here less than half an hour after I left you," she said, "I have to gather that the coaching was not a success. What happened?"

Several blunt statements jostled in my mind. But I settled for, "I don't think Mia wants to be coached."

"Did she give you the story of the two boarding schools?"

"Yes."

Mrs. Smith leaned against the wooden partition of the stall and stared down at the brush. "I investigated the school she's set her heart on. And I got three different reports, all saying that, while it had a good academic reputation, it had lately had trouble with drugs. It's near New York, the students have a lot of freedom, and that all adds up to an easy mark for dealers. We even have them in this town, as I'm sure you know."

"Yes," I said. But it wasn't that big a problem around the school, largely because parents, with the police helping them, made it their job to keep the school and its grounds under constant monitoring. "But they can't get to the students that easily," I said.

"I know. It's one of the ironies of this town that the public school has been better protected than the expensive establishment that Mia has gone to."

"Did she get into them herself?"

"A little. As far as I know only an occasional joint. But given her general state of rebellion I sure don't want to send her into a place like Broadhurst."

I went on brushing Toby, but asked, "Are you sure that the riding school you want to send her to is clear of all that stuff?"

"Today, nobody can be sure, but it's isolated in the country, most of the girls—for all I know, all of the girls—are horse-mad. It's not a guarantee, but I don't know of a better place."

"She hates horses."

"I know. I'm not trying to force her on one, Janet. But I think it would be better for her at least to try riding. She had a terrible fall about three years ago. She was in a cast for months. And she had a lot of pain."

"So it's a question of not wanting to get back on?" I knew that it was one of the iron traditions: if you fall from a horse or are thrown, get back on immediately— or as soon as possible. If you don't, you may never get back on.

She sighed. "At least in part. I take it she didn't tell you about it?"

22

I shook my head.

"I'd have felt better if she had. She won't even talk about it." There was a pause while I worked and she stood there. "What do you think?"

I looked down at the brush and started combing hairs out of it. "I don't think forcing a person to do something, or not to do something, works. If she doesn't want to ride, then she doesn't. Just the way forbidding me to ride . . ." It was at that moment that I remembered my lie of the previous day. I'd deliberately given Mrs. Smith the strong impression that Mother approved of my riding. Now she'd know it was all a fake. I stopped. There was another silence. Just suddenly I felt as though everything had fallen down on me. True, Mother had given me money for the Pony Club, but Mrs. Smith would now probably not let me stable Toby here, so what good would it do me? Everything stank.

"So your saying that your mother liked you to have outside activities, while not exactly a lie, wasn't exactly the truth, I take it."

"No."

"You really ought to switch mothers with Mia."

"I said that, too."

"You'd better hurry up with that if you want to fit in a lesson. Some of the Pony Club kids are coming around twelve and we're going trail riding in the state park."

"You mean you're going to coach me, anyway?"

"Yes." She said it abruptly. "Did your mother talk about her reasons for not wanting you to ride?"

"She thinks it's brainless, dangerous and for rich people."

Mrs. Smith laughed. "There's some truth in that, but not a lot. Let's hope she'll change." She walked down the stable, then turned as she reached Aldebaran. "Get your saddle on and let's go."

Fifty minutes of concentrated coaching later, Mrs. Smith said, "You're going to have to do a lot of hard work, but it will pay off. You're a natural rider, and you consider your horse, which is all important. All right, let's go back now and get ready for the Pony Clubbers. Somebody is bringing a contingent from the Abbot farms."

CHAPTER 4

Half an hour later the courtyard was filled with children of various ages and their ponies and horses of different sizes.

"All right now, kids," Mrs. Smith said, mounting Aldebaran, "we're going to do some trail riding in the park. Did you all bring sandwiches?"

There was a chorus of yeses, punctuated by a wail from a girl who looked about eleven.

"I forgot," she said.

"Don't forget next time, Pam. Luckily I've packed a few extra. Those jodhpurs look about two sizes too large for you."

"Brenda borrowed mine, so I borrowed Mike's."

"And what's Mike wearing?"

"He couldn't come. He's been grounded."

"Ah well, these things happen. Alan, are your lot all ready?"

I swung around, almost falling off Toby who was nibbling some grass near the edge of the yard. There, in jeans and khaki shirt, was Alan Grant.

Alan was the only subject on which Cynthia and Mother did not see eye to eye. Of all her numerous boyfriends, Mother liked him least. As she often said, "I just don't like the environment he comes from—rich and arrogant."

Mother might not like Alan, but Cynthia was not alone in her feeling. Along with half the girls in school, she had a crush on Alan Grant, captain of the hockey team, first string in tennis, on his inevitable way to Yale. He also, I had heard, had a horse, although he didn't seem to take much interest in it. And if that wasn't enough, he was Romeo to Cynthia's Juliet in the school Shakespeare festival. Still, he left me cold. I thought he was conceited and not very bright.

"Isn't he too old for the Pony Club?" I asked Mrs. Smith, who had Aldebaron brought over near me.

"He's an instructor today," she said. "Joe Burns, who usually goes out with us, has gone to the West Coast. So we won't have him. I called up Alan, thinking it was a lost cause, but he graciously said he'd come."

"Is he good enough?"

"As a matter of fact, he rides quite well—better than Joe, when he keeps his mind on it. The trouble is . . . Well, that's not anything to bother you with right now. But don't worry. We'll have him or somebody like him whenever we go out. I need more than just myself. Okay, everybody, let's go through that gate, and we'll head towards the bridge."

It was a beautiful summer day, and I was so delighted to be a member of the club and out with other riders that the time went like lightning. We climbed up the highest of the nearby hills, and then down again, and tethered the horses to various trees and bushes while we sat down and ate our sandwiches. Some mothers had showed up on their own horses. Others had driven into the park, had left their cars on one of the lay-bys and walked across the fields. They put down blankets and produced cookies and sodas and thermos flasks of coffee and tea and fruit juice. It was nice to see them involved that way. I tried to imagine Mother doing the same and couldn't. I knew she played tennis and squash at a local racquet club with other professional men and women. But it wasn't the same thing at all. I sat around a blanket with a boy of about twelve and two girls of about thirteen. They were nice. I knew one girl slightly from school, but had never seen the other who, it turned out, went to the same school as Mia.

Towards the end of lunch, Alan strolled over and sat down. "That's a nice pony," he said, looking at Toby who was tethered to a low branch of a tree and was munching grass.

Since the Grants could buy any horse they wanted, I knew he must be being sarcastic.

"Wither him with your contempt," Fantasy George whispered, his blue eyes blazing, his steel armor shimmering in the sunlight.

I said coldly, "Even though he comes from a long line of peasants, he suits me."

"Why the ruffles? I wasn't being sarcastic. He really is nice. Reminds me of my first pony."

"I paid two hundred dollars for him."

"So what? Is that the only way you judge a horse?"

"Of course not. I just meant . . ." Since I wasn't quite sure what I meant, but was fairly certain that whatever it was, it wouldn't be considered complimentary, I stopped.

"You just meant that rich types like me only judge by the bottom line. Right?"

"Well, you never said you were particularly keen on riding."

"I wasn't. But I'm beginning to think I might take it up again."

"Why?"

"For the pleasure of ruffling your feathers."

"Why don't you concentrate on Cynthia?"

"Because she doesn't ruffle as satisfactorily." He jumped to his feet. "Time to go."

I told Cynthia that Alan Grant was instructing with the Pony Club.

She shrugged. "I thought the kids there would be too young to interest him."

"I think he was helping out. Mrs. Smith needed help. She says he rides well. Even though I don't like him much, I have to admit he does."

"Why don't you like him?"

"Because I can't stand that attitude of his—you know what I mean: 'I'm ruler of all I survey'."

She giggled a little. "Including and especially all the women."

"You like him, don't you, Cyn?"

She shrugged again. "I really haven't thought much about him."

I opened my mouth to say something like "What a lie," or "Tell me another," when I remembered that I owed her one.

"Who do you like?" Cynthia asked. "By the time I was your age I'd already had a crush on two boys."

"And at least four had a crush on you."

"Yes," she agreed happily.

"Well, in that you're fulfilling Mother's master plan."

"I know. But I don't think it's the big deal you think it is. If I turned out to want to do something other than what Mom wants, then she'd go along. Like I told you, she's not unreasonable. You'll see."

"Maybe she'd go along with you. She wouldn't with me. She likes you better than she does me."

"Jan—that's a terrible thing to say!"

"I've said it before."

"Not for a long time, and I thought you'd grown out of it. It's not true."

"Yes, it is."

I knew right away that I would have done better to have kept my mouth shut. "It's okay," I said hastily. "It doesn't matter."

"If you think that then it does matter. But I think it's only because Mom doesn't like you spending all that time at the horse farm. And I agree with her."

"You were the one who told her that she was being unfair—remember?"

"Sure. And in that instance, she was. But she hates you being so besotted about that horse. She feels you ought to have other interests, and so do I. I personally think it'd be much better for you to be besotted about a boyfriend. I bet every girl in your class has one."

"What if they do? I'm barely fourteen."

"Time's a-flying! You're just socially immature. And mucking out horse manure heaven knows how many hours a week isn't going to do anything for you."

"I can't believe this! You stuck up for me!"

Cynthia suddenly shouted. "Well I'm not sticking up for you any more on that subject. And please leave me alone. Don't you have anything else to do?"

"Yes. Plenty!"

"Well go and do it! After all, this is my room!"

"So sorry, ma'am!" I made a mock bow and went up to my room in the attic.

The next day at school I slid into the desk next to Morris Blair. Until Toby, Morris came the nearest to being my best friend, maybe because we're both mis-fits—me because I feel different from the others and am

tongue-tied around them, Morris because he's the
school math genius. He's way ahead of the rest of the
class and takes math with the seniors, although in the
other subjects he's only a little beyond the rest of us.
Things at school aren't always easy for him, either.
Sometimes the jocks call him "Meow," because of Morris the cat. But it doesn't seem to bother him. Once I
asked him why.

"Because I like cats," he said and grinned.

Morris was now poking at his pocket calculator.

"What are you doing?" I asked. "Computing the
density of the earth?"

"That's already been done," he said scornfully.
"I'm trying something else."

"Like what?"

"Like the ratio of the distance from the earth to
Mars as a relative adaptable to the galaxy."

It made no sense to me as I'm sure he knew. I
glanced quickly at him to see if he was looking amused.
But his glasses were so thick you couldn't tell.

"Of course," I said. "Let me know when you've
worked it out."

He smiled, baring his steel braces. "I will. By the
way," he said, "I've got an extra ticket for an astronomy
show at the natural history museum. D'you want to
go?"

"When is it?"

"Right after school."

"Regretfully I shook my head. "Can't. Have to go
and muck out. I'm sorry."

"Well . . ." He took some tickets out of his pocket
and looked at them. "They're good for two weeks. And
there are lots of showings. When can you?"

I thought. "I can go Sunday morning, but maybe
you can't make it."

"They have a showing at ten. We can do it then." He stared at me. "But are you telling me you're busy every afternoon and all of Sunday?"

"Between the barn and babysitting, yes."

"Don't you get fed up with it? With being over-scheduled?"

"No. I like doing it. Do you get fed up with reading scientific stuff?"

"No. But it's funny. My mom would give a lot if I developed even one athletic pursuit. She's convinced I'm going to die of muscular entropy." Another link between Morris and me is that his mother is the Angela Blair who works in Mother's office as her secretary and walks on crutches.

"Why do all mothers want you to be something else? Why can't they be satisfied with what you are?"

"Oh, Mom isn't so bad. And she's right, from the point of view of health."

I said suddenly, "You don't have a father, do you?"

"Nope."

"Is your mother divorced?"

"No. Dad died in an accident just after I was born. He never saw me."

"And your mother hasn't married since, or anything?"

"I'm not sure about the anything, although I don't think so. But she certainly hasn't married. She gets a pension from some insurance Dad had. But it's not a lot, so that's why she's always worked. Not that she probably wouldn't want to, anyway."

"I was just thinking about our mothers. They're the same, yet they're different. Of course, I haven't met your mother."

"Well, come over after the astronomy show."

"How long will it last?"

"About an hour."

"The Pony Club meets around two-thirty, so I guess I can. I'm just not too sure how the lessons are going to work out, if they are."

"What's the problem?"

I told him about Mia and the coaching arrangement and how it fell through. "So, since Mia won't let herself be coached, I don't know whether Mrs. Smith's going to give me another lesson."

"Umm," he said. "I've heard about Mia Smith. She's supposed to be wild."

"How do you know? She doesn't go to school here."

"One of the kids in the science club knows her. Did you like her?"

I thought for a moment. Despite the fact that it looked as though she had put an end to my coaching lessons, my main feeling was that she was grossly unhappy. "I don't know whether I like her or not. I'd have to see her when she wasn't being one huge, negative lump."

"Want to meet me at the museum Sunday morning? Or do you want me to call for you?"

I thought instantly of my conversation with Cynthia. And for a moment I thought how nice it would be to have Morris come and pick me up. Then I got pigheaded. Why should I try to create an untrue impression just to impress Mother and Cynthia.

"No," I said. "You live on the other side of town."

"It's not that far, for heaven's sake!"

"I'll meet you at the museum. And thanks!"

32

Sunday morning, around eight, I was sitting at the kitchen table munching some cereal when Mother came downstairs. She was in a rose-colored robe and her hair was mussed up. I thought she looked much prettier that way than she did in her gray flannel suit and briefcase. It seems funny to say she was "in" her brief-case as though it were part of her clothing, but since I never saw her leave or come home without it, it might as well have been.

"I guess I don't have to ask where you're going," she said in her flat morning voice.

For a moment I didn't respond. Part of me, the puppy-dog-in-need-of-love part, wanted to reassure her that I was not going to the barn, that I was going to the museum, and furthermore I was going with a boy. The other side despised me for being so eager to please.

She sat down. "If you spent all that energy and time in something useful you'd probably end up as the first woman president."

"If I did you'd manage to find something wrong with it," I said. I got up and took my cereal bowl to the sink and rinsed it out. The kettle started to scream. I poured it into the filter of the drip pot Mother had set up the night before.

"I hope that wasn't a serious comment," Mother said.

I didn't want to start a fight, so I waited a few moments, then poured the coffee into a mug and took it to her. "I'm going to meet Morris Blair at the museum to see the astronomy show.

She sipped the coffee. "Angela Blair's son?"

"Yes."

"What's he like? From the picture on her desk he looks all glasses and nose."

"He's not going to win the Hunk of the Week Contest, but he's bright and funny, and I like him. In fact, he's so brilliant in math that he's way ahead of us. He takes math with the seniors."

Mother put down her cup. "That's funny."

"What?"

"That Angela never mentioned that. I'd have thought she'd have bragged all over the place."

"Why?"

"Well, she's only a—" Mother paused. "That didn't come out quite the way I meant it."

"You mean because she's only a secretary among you hot-shot lawyers. That's pretty snobbish, isn't it?" Mother and I looked at one another. "Almost as bad as the horsey set."

There was a tense pause, then Mother gave a shout of laughter and the hard edge between us seemed to go away. "You're right. I'm sorry, Jan." She got up, gave me a hug and started out of the kitchen carrying her mug. At the door she turned. "When can we have the honor of seeing you this evening?"

"Around six, I guess. I'm going to be doing some coaching, then some work around the barn and then have a lesson. After that, it's Pony Club."

34

Mother waved. "All right. If you're not home by seven I'll send out the marines."

Morris was waiting for me just inside the main hall. He was busy reading some material and didn't see me. I looked at him, remembering Mother's comment about his looking "all glasses and nose," and decided that while he did have a prominent nose it was aquiline and well-shaped, and his glasses suited him. In fact, he was quite good-looking. I walked up to him. "Hi!"

He looked up over his pamphlet. "Oh, there you are. Hi! This looks like it ought to be a good show. Let's get some decent seats."

"What's it going to be about?" I asked him when we sat down. We were in a small round auditorium with a domed ceiling.

"About the planets and how they move and shift with the seasons." He looked at me. "Do you know anything about astronomy?"

"Only that I'm a Gemini."

"Come on! You know better than that! That's astrology. Fit for con men and silly women.

"Only women?"

He grinned. "Don't get your feminism in an uproar. Most of the letters in the newspaper to Madame Nadia are from women. Don't you ever read her column?"

"Yes," I admitted. It was true, nearly all the letters were signed by female names.

"But," Morris went on, "it's true that once—about two thousand years ago—astronomy and astrology were considered the same thing."

"What made them different?"

"The advance in mathematics. Also religion. The Church more or less threw it out."

"What Church?"

"The Catholic Church through the medieval period. After that, most of the churches."

At that moment a middle-aged man in a blue suit walked out into the center of the auditorium. "Good morning," he said pleasantly. "The show you're going to see this afternoon is called 'The Dance of the Heavenly Bodies.' I hope very much you'll enjoy it. Now we'll put out the lights and you'll see that the ceiling simulates the night sky."

I hadn't really expected to like it much, but I found the next hour fascinating.

"Well?" Morris asked when the lights went up.

"It was terrific!"

He grinned. "I thought you'd like it. By the way, Mom wants you to come back for coffee and cake. Can you?"

I glanced at my watch. It was about ten minutes past ten. "Sure. I'll have to leave no later than about quarter past eleven, because I have a coaching session at twelve-thirty." We went outside.

"We can get a bus here." Morris indicated a stop sign. "Are you being coached, or are you coaching Mia?"

"Trying to coach Mia is more like it. At least I have to show up and make the effort. If she throws me out again—well, I'll have tried."

"As we got into the bus Morris said, "Is this to pay for your riding lessons?"

"That's right."

When we got off I saw we were in the older part of the town where the houses were attached. We walked up some outside steps and through a door. Morris inserted

36

his key and we went into a hall. There he used another key to open another door into his apartment. I had the impression of polished wood floors and high ceilings and a pleasant, flowery smell. Then I looked up and saw a woman approaching us.

In a way it was like looking at Morris—except, of course, for her crutches. She was tall and slender and had dark wavy brown hair the way he did, and she also wore glasses.

"It's Janet, isn't it?" she said, holding out her hand.

"Yes." For some reason I was stricken with shyness.

She indicated the sofa and chairs in the living room. "Shall we sit down? Morris, the food is ready. Why don't you bring it in?" She walked over to an armchair, rested her crutches against the side and sat down.

For some reason I couldn't keep my eyes off her crutches. She noticed my glance and smiled. "The result of an accident years ago. It's annoying, but at this point in my life, nothing worse. Morris tells me you're involved with the Pony Club."

I was surprised, but tried not to show it. "Yes. I've just joined. It's great! Are you familiar with it?"

"I certainly am. I was even a member. But then, as they say, life intervened and I had to do other things."

At that point Morris came into the living room carrying a tray containing coffee and some cake which he put down on a low table in front of his mother. I laughed. "I like that—'life intervened.' "

She picked up a white china coffee pot and started to pour. "Isn't that about it? We make marvelous and intricate plans and then life—in the form of something wonderful, or something terrible, or something that isn't one or the other but is still demanding—makes us throw out the plan and start from scratch. Milk?"

"Yes, please."

"Sugar?"

"No thanks."

I got up, took the cup and a plate of cake she was holding out, and then sat down again.

"And you're coaching, too. Mia Smith, I believe."

"Do you know her?"

"No." She smiled. "I hear of her through Morris who knows some of the people she goes to school with."

I hesitated before blurting out what was on the tip of my tongue. "She had some kind of an accident—riding accident, I've been told."

Mrs. Blair looked at me through her clear gray eyes—eyes very like her son's. "I've heard that, too. As I know, it can have a daunting effect on one's riding."

"Was yours a riding accident?" I couldn't stop my curiosity.

"Yes, it was. Entirely my own fault, too. I got stupidly obstinate about riding a certain horse I'd been told not to."

"So you never rode again?" I asked slowly, thinking of Mia.

"I couldn't. I woke up in the hospital. After that, it was a year of so of physical therapy before I was able to walk." She smiled. "Having to walk with these"—she indicated her crutches—"is, believe it or not, a triumph, not a calamity. It could have been far worse. But that was long ago. Let's talk about something else."

There was a pause. Then she said, "I hear your sister, Cynthia, is going to be Juliet in the play."

It shouldn't have upset me, of course, something I reminded myself of every time somebody mentioned Cynthia and pushed in front of me the fact that I've always lived in her shadow. But somehow I hadn't expected it here with Morris and his mother—least of all with Morris and his mother. Mrs. Blair might work in Mother's office, but they were my discovery, my friends, apart from Mother and her office and Cynthia. Suddenly my heart started to beat and I felt a familiar sensation—wanting to get away.

"Yes," I said and remembered Cynthia telling me to get out of her room. "She's also brainy." I put down my coffee and got up. "I'm terribly sorry. I have to go now. I have to go home and pick up my bike and—"

"Do you have to go?" Mrs. Blair asked. Her gray eyes were puzzled. "I—both Morris and I hoped you could stay for at least another fifteen minutes. Then I can drive you to the stables."

"But I have to have my bike to come home on. Please don't bother. Thank you so much. Thanks a lot, Morris."

I ran down the outside steps and was almost at the avenue before I heard Morris's voice. "Hey! Come back a minute! What's the matter with you?"

But I didn't stop. When I got to the avenue I turned and waved. "See you at school." Then I ran across the avenue, against the lights, ignoring the horns honking at me and the yells of drivers. The bus going towards my house was just about ready to leave, but I scrambled in.

"That's a good way to get killed," the driver said.

"I'm late," I replied, putting money in the box.

"Better late than dead or mangled."

When he said the word, "mangled," I had a sudden visual image of Mrs. Blair coming off her horse, and the horse falling on top of her. And I saw Mia doing the same. I closed my eyes. From the first time I had thrown a leg over a horse at the age of nine—it was just a farm horse, but that ride changed my life—I had known no fear. I knew what could happen. I had seen people fall and get thrown. But I was quite sure that I could handle anything my horse did. Was all this talk about falls going to rob me of that?

I looked down to see my hands clenched.

"I thought you said you wanted to get off here?" the bus driver said. The bus had stopped and the driver was looking at me through his rearview mirror.

"Come on, kid. Don't keep the bus waiting," one of the passengers chimed in.

I sprang up. "Sorry!" I muttered, then ran to the front of the bus and got out. I looked at my watch. It was eleven. My stomach growled a little, sounding loud in the Sunday silence. I had planned to eat something before going to the barn, such as Mrs. Blair's cake. But I hadn't, so instead of just taking my bike out of the garage, I ought to go into the house and make a sandwich or eat a bun.

I ran along the road to our house, then went straight through the back door into the kitchen. Cynthia was there reading the Sunday paper funnies. "Thought you were out with your boyfriend," she said.

I opened up the refrigerator. "I was."

"Was he too cheap to feed you?"

I decided I was tired of the jibes that had been coming my way lately. "Why don't you get off my back?"

There was some cold chicken inside the refrigerator. I brought it out and pulled off a drumstick. Then I took a couple of slices of bread from the bread box, buttered them, and started eating the chicken and the bread. I poured a glass of milk to go with the rest and stood at the kitchen counter gulping it all down.

"Mom says that Mrs. Blair is the perfect secretary," Cynthia said and added, "whatever that means."

There was a jumble in my head, mixing up a lot of things. In our town the rich people lived in one of the

40

outer suburbs and did most of the riding. They either owned their own stables and horses, or they kept their horses in one of two rich horse farms. Those were the people Mother resented and talked about when she mentioned "the horsey set." Mrs. Smith had one good horse, Aldebaran, which she rode in shows. But Smith farm was far less formal, its fees smaller and its atmosphere more relaxed than the other, bigger horse farms. And the Pony Club was filled with kids of more modest backgrounds. But they still had their own horses, which put them in the category Mother disapproved of because she thought of them as snobbish.

But wasn't her comment about Mrs. Blair also snobbish?

"I don't know why you're so defensive." Cynthia turned the page. "Snapping my head off merely because I asked if Morris was a cheap date."

"You've snapped my head off a lot lately, remember? You also told me to get out of your room."

Cynthia shrugged. "Don't push your luck."

"What do you mean by that?"

She didn't say anything; she seemed absorbed in the paper.

A little quiver of fear went through me. "What do you mean?"

Cynthia got up slowly. "Mom's going all out over this take-over thing. She'll be the first woman partner in a law firm in this town, and she's not going to be happy if something takes her time and attention away from it." And she trailed out of the kitchen, taking the paper with her.

CHAPTER 6

I cleaned out Toby's stall, talking to him in a low voice, and got fresh water for him and some of the other horses.

"I don't know why people have to have attitudes towards horses," I muttered to him. "I don't have an attitude towards Cyrus."

Cyrus, a large, fuzzy ginger cat, was a great friend of Toby's and I would often find him sleeping in Toby's stall. Cyrus rubbed against my leg, and I bent down and patted him.

Being with Toby soothed me, as it always did. After a while, brushing him, I was able to look at what had happened at the Blair's. I drew the brush slowly down his side. "It isn't as though people didn't always say something about Cynthia. My chief claim to fame," I muttered gloomily to myself, "being her sister." But never before had I acted that way. I knew it was rude and felt mortified. "It was because she was Morris's mother," I told Toby, stroking his neck. I just hasn't expected it from that direction. Morris was my friend, my first real date. Cynthia's jibing voice filled my mind. "Was he too cheap to feed you?"

"Who cares?" I said aloud. Then I kissed Toby on his forehead and went off to get the wheelbarrow for the other stalls.

At twelve-thirty I went into the house and up the stairs and walked along the hall to Mia's room. I knew I was going more to prove to myself that I was at least trying to earn my riding lessons than with any belief that Mia would let me open a book.

So I was surprised when Mia turned as I came in and indicated the card table that was in the middle of the room with two chairs. "Have a seat," she said.

I sat down. On the table were two books, one a French grammar and one a standard text of English and American poetry.

To say I was amazed would be putting it mildly. I decided not to ask any questions but to go along as things presented themselves. "Are these the texts you've been told to study?"

She remained standing. "Yes."

The next question had to be asked. "By which school?"

Her smile was sarcastic. "Need you ask? The school Ma wants me to go to."

I looked up at her, "Okay. Let's go. We'll start with the French book."

I suppose I expected her to balk at every step of the way, certainly in view of the fact that she had refused even to consider coaching. But she came over to the table, perhaps a little grudgingly, and sat down.

She was certainly not stupid. I had constantly to remind myself that however unwillingly she cooperated, however peevishly she snapped, she actually learned quickly, answered my questions immediately and well and retained the rules governing French grammar that I laid out.

I was dying to ask her what changed her mind, but something held me back. We worked quite well for an hour. Then she stretched up her arms and said, "Time's up. That's enough for today. Anyway, you have to go for your riding lesson." She glanced at me from under her long lashes. "Isn't that right?"

I got up. "Yes. It is." I turned at the door. "See you next time!"

She was still sitting at the table, one arm crooked over the back of her chair. Suddenly she grinned, "Do you think there's any hope for me?"

I hesitated, not wanting to press my luck. Then I smiled, "Your French isn't so bad, but I still have to see your English." Her mother's words sounded in the back of my mind: "When she writes she sounds like an illiterate."

"Don't tell me. Let me guess—Ma told you I was a cretin at writing."

"She didn't say that."

"No? Something like it, I bet! Well, don't let me keep you from the Pony Club. You know what Pony stands for?"

I shook my head.

"The Putrid Organization of Nerdlike Yahoos."

Curiously, as though it were a movie in my mind, I saw the horse with her on it, capping a fence and then missing the angle of the slope underneath and falling, falling, with her underneath. "There's nothing wrong with your vocabulary," I said finally.

"What's the matter? You look funny."

"Nothing. See you tomorrow." I went down to the barn where Mrs. Smith was waiting for me.

Later that afternoon at the Pony Club rally we had a game. There were stanchions down one of the fields and we rode our horses zigzagging between. If we touched a stanchion, it was one fault. If we knocked it down it was two. Whichever of two teams ran the course

44

in the shortest time with the least number of faults won. Mrs. Smith took one team and Alan the other. I was in Alan's team, and before the game actually started, he ran us through the course a couple of times, knowing some of us hadn't done this before.

"Okay, you guys," Alan said. He was riding a palomino and had on a straw cowboy hat. "I know whoever does it fastest with the least faults wins. But I'd rather you'd concentrate on not knocking over or even touching a stanchion, and, most of all, not tugging on your bits so as to damage your horses' mouths. Janet, why don't you start the practice?"

"I've never done it before," I protested, not wanting to look a complete fool in front of everybody.

"So? Everybody has to begin some time. Now get moving!"

I was furious and decided that for some reason Alan wanted to make me look silly. Angrily, I wheeled Toby out of the lineup and trotted him through the zigzag course.

"All right," Alan said. "Now you know the course, so canter!"

Somehow Toby and I got through without knocking down one of the stanchions. I did brush one, however, and it quivered for a moment, but held.

"That's not bad," Alan said, "but you're going to have to bring your horse about faster than that. Judy, you next!"

Judy's pants were almost as beat up as mine and her boots were worse, since mine were almost new. All this, plus the way she sat her pony, told me she'd had experience riding. I was right. She and her mount, a gray mare, whisked through the course with dispatch and without touching the stanchions.

"Okay," Alan said. "Now you, Burt."

A red-haired boy who looked about eleven wheeled his pony to the beginning of the course.

"Alan's certainly stingy with his praise," I said to Judy. "You were better than okay."

She grinned. "Thanks, but I think he thinks he can't say anything nice about me."

"Why?" I asked, more than ready to take offense.

"Because he's my cousin."

"You don't live here, do you? At least, you don't go to the local public school."

"No. I live with Mother in Bedford, outside New York. My parents are divorced."

"Are you going to visit here long?"

"I'll be here for the year. Mom's remarried and her husband is head of a news bureau in London. I wanted to go with her but she said it wouldn't be convenient for me to be with them right away." She sounded both angry and sad.

"And your father's here?"

"He's moving back here. He's Aunt Jessica's brother, you know." When I look puzzled she added, "Jessica Smith. Of Smith Farm," she finished up and laughed. "You didn't know her first name?"

"No, I didn't. Are you going to stay on the farm?"

"For a while. It's half Dad's. But Aunt Jessica managed it for him while he was on the coast."

"It'll be neat to have you. Are you coming to the public school or to Miss Mary's?"

"I don't know yet."

"It must be nice to have a male cousin, like an older brother," I said. Or like a father, I silently added.

"Well, it is. Though Alan can sometimes be a pain in the neck. I guess all male siblings or cousins can. I'll say this, they're better than fathers!"

She said it with anger. For a moment neither of us spoke. Then I said, "I wouldn't know."

Our team won, even though Burt and I managed to knock over three stanchions.

"That wasn't bad at all," Alan said, "considering it was your first time."

"It was awful." I leaned over and patted Toby. "But we'll get better."

"How're you going home?" he asked.

"By bike. After I've finished unsaddling Toby and grooming him."

"Sparky here is going home in the trailer," he said, stroking his horse, "which one of the grooms is driving. So I can give you a lift in my car."

"But I have my bike here."

"We can put it in the back seat."

For a moment, I had a wonderful vision of me driving up to the house with Alan, with Cynthia looking out the window and seeing us. Then I looked at Toby, straining to get to some grass at the edge of the path. He was worth anything, including not making Cynthia mad. Because if she got mad, Mother would be, too. It wasn't fair, but it was the way it was.

"Okay?" Alan said.

"Thanks. But I think I'd rather bike home." And I turned Toby's head towards the barn.

The next Pony Club rally was on the following Saturday at the Grants' farm. Toby, of course, would go in a trailer with the other horses. But it was too far for me to go on my bike, so I had to figure out a way to get there. The obvious course would be for me to ask

Mother or Cynthia to drive me. But the hazards were equally obvious: Mother would hold it against Toby, and, because it was the home of Alan Grant, Cynthia would almost certainly bite my head off. There were no other kids at school that I was sure were going. This left Mrs. Smith, who would undoubtedly be driving one of the trailers. But since I wasn't sure of my status with her on account of Mia's changeable attitudes, I hesitated to ask for extra favors.

While I worked around the barn that evening after school, I kept an eye out for Mrs. Smith. Finally, when I was just about finishing up, she came out of the house. "Have you seen Terry?" she asked.

Terry Low was one of the people she taught. She went to Miss Mary's so I didn't know her very well, but she always struck me as a little flaky. I shook my head.

"She's due here for a lesson, but I've been watching the front, and I haven't seen her drive up." Mrs. Smith walked past me to Bambi's stall. "Bambi's stall looks pretty clean, so I take it that you did it. Terry's more inclined to hide the dirty sawdust under the clean than to change it—that is, when she thinks she can get away with it." She sighed. "And that means that Bambi hasn't been exercised properly today."

"I can take her out after I finish with Toby," I said.

"No. I'll exercise her later. Right now I'm going to take you to the ring. You need some dressage schooling."

It was so unexpected I felt the tears spring to my eyes. Here was somebody I didn't have to plead with or tiptoe around. "Thanks," I muttered, with my back to Mrs. Smith. She was such a cool, reserved person, I didn't want her to think I was some kind of tearful wimp. It seemed insanity, but I decided to get my doubts out into the open. "I've only been able to give Mia one lesson so far."

"Do what you can with her, but don't worry about it. You have the makings of a really good rider, and I can use your help in the club, especially with some of the younger children. Come along now!"

To my astonishment I felt her hand on my shoulder. I turned. The cool blue eyes were warm and smiling. My heart gave a jump. I cleared my throat. "Thanks," I muttered again, inadequately.

We worked on trotting for awhile, then she put up one of the hurdles to a low eighteen inches. "Have you jumped?"

"No," I said, my heart beating.

"Well, come towards it slowly. Toby will know better than you what he should do. Remember, lean forward as he rises to the jump."

It felt strange at first. And when he cleared the jump and came down the other side I was sure I'd come off. But by some miracle I didn't.

"That was good. Now let's try it again, and don't clutch the rein quite so hard."

"At the end of the hour I felt both exhilarated and tired. I took Toby on a quick, twenty-minute workout around the reservoir in the near part of the park and then brought him back. Mrs. Smith was cleaning out Aldebaran's stall when I led Toby into the stable.

"Your mother called," she said as I passed. "Apparently the people for whom you babysit telephoned her, wondering where you were."

I stood, feeling as though I'd turned to stone. I'd entirely forgotten that the Turners had asked me to come early as they were going to a special dinner.

"I forgot about it," I said. "Oh Lord!" This would

be grist to Mother's mill. I could almost hear her voice, "Just as I was afraid of, Janet, you're spending so much time at that wretched barn that you forgot your obligations and let down people who are depending on you." It was hard not to believe that she was standing next to me saying that. "I'll call as soon as I get home," I said. And then, "I wonder if they found somebody."

"From what your mother said, they did." Mrs. Smith hesitated. "I'm sorry. I think I distracted you."

"I'm not sorry. I'd a million times rather be doing something here than babysitting."

"In that case, I can use you for as much time as you have to give, and I'll pay you the going rate!"

"That would be absolutely wonderful!" I said, hardly able to believe my luck. "Thanks a lot!"

"By the way, I asked your mother if she were coming to the picnic on Saturday. I thought I might stir up her interest a little, but I'm afraid it had the opposite effect. Again, my apologies. I didn't make things easier for you. Do you have any idea why she's as opposed to riding as she is?"

I shook my head. "No." I got the saddle off Toby and put it up outside on his stand. As I went back in I said, "She seems to think it's terribly, well, snobbish. And then she always brings up her secretary, Mrs. Blair, being lame because of a riding accident."

Mrs. Smith was standing in the stall door, having settled Aldebaran in his stall several yards beyond. "Are you talking about Angela Blair?"

"Yes. Do you know her?"

"I used to see her riding. She rode very well indeed, and then she had that terrible accident."

"Does it bother you—the accidents people have?"

"It bothers me in the sense that it's an appalling thing to happen to anybody. But if you mean, does it make me afraid, the answer is no. No more than I am afraid when I get into a car, even though the statistical chance of an accident on the road is far higher than on my horse." She looked at me. "Why? Does it bother you?"

"Not any more," I said and knew it to be the truth. But I also knew that in the past week I had been afraid. "I was, but I'm not now."

"I've always thought that people who claim they don't know the meaning of the word 'fear' when on a horse are either dumb or dead from the neck up. However much you love your horse, it's still a thousand-pound animal that can take fright, bolt, fall, and/or roll over you. But knowing that something can be true—especially if you know what you're doing—and letting it haunt you, are two different things."

"Yes," I said. "I understand now."

Mrs. Smith was staring down at the brush in her hands. "I hope I haven't made things more difficult for you. To some extent what your mother says is true. The horsey world is filled with upwardly mobile people who are using it to launch themselves and their children into a higher social bracket. I've always found it a little nauseating, especially when I'm asked to teach a child who would rather be anywhere else, is terrified of horses, but is held there by the social ambitions of her mother. It's harder on the child, but often much harder on the horse. But then there are the same climbers in the world of ballet and art. A lot of people use those volunteer groups supporting the arts of one kind or another to meet the so-called 'right people' and to launch themselves into the 'right'—in quotes—society. But nobody suggests that we abolish art and ballet." She hesitated, then bent down and picked up Cyrus, who had padded in to be with his friend, Toby.

I collected the harness and gave Toby a final pat. "Is Cyrus supposed to catch mice?"

"Theoretically. And I think he does from time to time, because he comes into the house and proudly gives me a dead mouse. But he gets his share of delicacies at home, too." She paused. "How are you getting to the Grants on Saturday?"

"I don't know. I haven't figured it out yet. It's really too far to bike."

"Well, you can bike here and come in the trailer with me."

CHAPTER 7

Riding over with Mrs. Smith in the trailer on Saturday was wonderful. "What's going to happen?" I asked. "I mean, when we get there?"

"The Grants have a number of large fields, more than anyone in the area. In one of them Pony Club members like you who are still unrated will be put through dressage tests, jumping, and asked questions about horse care and feed." She glanced at me. "You probably know a fair amount about that."

"Yes. I mostly just give Toby the feed that comes in the sacks, but I do know that it should be sweet feed— oats, corn and molasses."

"That's right. But you'd be surprised at the number of people who keep expensive horses but who know and care zero about what their animal eats. For all they know we could be giving them banana splits."

I giggled. "As a matter of fact, once when I was out with Toby, somebody had brought some ice cream and cones. I gave him some in a cone and he loved it."

"Aldebaran here likes colas, but I don't let him have too many. A horse can develop a sweet tooth, just like us, and just like us have to watch it."

The Grants' farm, Wildwood, was enormous. After

we turned into their property, we seemed to drive for ages down an avenue of trees, with rolling pastures on either side and horses grazing everywhere.

"How many horses do the Grants have?" I asked.

"Probably twenty, but I know they stable some other people's, too. You know Alan Grant, don't you?"

"Actually, Cynthia, my sister, knows him better. Or would like to." That last part came out without my thinking about it. "I guess I shouldn't have said that," I said. "I didn't really mean to."

"I wouldn't worry too much. Cynthia is only one of a horde of interested damsels. Haven't you noticed a sudden increase in the number of female riders every time Alan is helping out?"

I hadn't particularly, but the moment she mentioned it I knew it was true. "Yes, now that you mention it. But I can't see it myself."

"You mean you're impervious to the Grant charm? That really makes you an original. Is there anybody who does stir your heart?"

"Not really. I like Morris Blair. I went to the planetarium with him last week. That's when I met his mother. But I don't feel anything like that—like Cynthia does about Alan."

"Never mind. One day you'll fall in love with somebody and be just as boring on the subject as anyone else. More so, maybe, to make up for lost time. In the meantime, don't worry about it." Then she turned and smiled, and I knew everything was going to be all right.

"Your mother would tell you the same," she added. My buzz of happiness faded abruptly.

"No she wouldn't," I said, hearing the anger in my voice. And then added, "She doesn't like me." To my knowledge I'd never thought that before, let alone said it. I'd known I wasn't the favorite, but that wasn't the

54

same thing. However, the moment the words were out, I knew they were true.

"Janet, that's a terrible thing to say, and I'm sure you must be wrong."

"I know it's a terrible thing to say. But I'm not wrong. She likes Cynthia better than me."

We drove for a while in silence, the trees flying past. Some of them were so tall and leafy that they met overhead. I put my head forward and up to see the roof they made to the road. Also to keep Mrs. Smith from knowing that I was having a hard time not crying. And now Mrs. Smith will think I'm a disloyal jerk, I thought. "You probably think I shouldn't have said that."

"No, don't think that!" She hesitated. "I guess I was having . . . the standard mother's response. Also, as you were talking, I was hearing your words in Mia's mouth."

I had forgotten about Mia. In a curious way, the more Mrs. Smith became my friend, the less I thought about her as Mia's mother. Yet always before, in any parent-kid fight among my friends, I was automatically on the kid's side. Now I wasn't. "What was Mia like before the accident? I mean, did the drugs and everything start afterwards?"

"Yes, although I have resisted thinking that it all sprang from the accident."

"Why? Why don't you want to think it came from the fall?"

Suddenly from behind some trees, the house came into view. Mrs. Smith slowed the car. "Because I've always, to some extent, felt responsible. Mia never really took to riding. I didn't think I was pushing her, but from everything she says now, she thinks I did." There was another silence. We rolled slowly forward. "You see," Mrs. Smith said lightly, "I was right. You and Mia should have switched mothers. Come along. We have to get parked properly and get the horses out."

I was riding Toby towards the arena when I was stunned to see Cynthia talking to Alan. They were standing in a small clearing entirely surrounded by excited Pony Club members both on and off horses, a clutch of mothers carrying hampers of one kind or another, and various Pony Club officials, probably there to rate new members like me.

For a moment I considered pretending I hadn't seen Cynthia. Then I decided she'd tell Mother I'd been rude. So I simply said, "Hi!" as I rode past.

"Hi, Jan," Cynthia said so nicely I was immediately suspicious. "I didn't know you were going to be here today. You should have told me."

All that sweetness and charm, of course, was for Alan's benefit, and it made me feel sick. Maybe, I thought, this was the reason I didn't get a crush on some boy, because of the power of negative example. Cynthia and I had never been friends. We'd hadn't had much of a relationship of any kind, really. But I'd never seen her so phony. I wanted to lash out with some really angry comment, but I didn't dare. Cynthia would tell Mother, and Mother would immediately decide it was because I was paying too much attention to Toby. Sitting there, with the April warm sun beating down on my arms, I had a great longing to be somebody else, with different parents. I wouldn't have then to go pussyfooting around, always afraid that if I said what I really felt about anything, then I'd be grounded and forbidden to ride. One day, I thought angrily, I'd be free. I'd do what I want and say what I want. No one would have a hold on me.

"Well," Alan said and grinned. "Cat got your tongue?"

"I didn't know you wanted to come," I said finally to Cynthia. I had pulled Toby up and was sitting there with the reins on his neck.

"So this is the great Toby," Cynthia said. She walked up to me, but approached from Toby's hindquarters. Now Toby is an angel, but like most horses he doesn't like people coming up on him from the rear. So he snorted and stamped and wheeled away. He wasn't about to kick her, but I could see Cynthia stop and back away.

"What's the matter with him?" she asked, sounding arrogant. I should have remembered that that simply meant she was scared, and I might have if she hadn't added, "Whatever you paid for him, the price was too high!"

I don't know what I would have replied, but luckily, or perhaps unluckily, I was forestalled by Alan. "That's a good horse, Cynthia. And if you come to a horse rally, you ought to learn a few simple rules about how to behave. Any horse will resent your walking up to his rear like that."

There was a gasp and a muffled giggle. I looked over towards the sound. It came from Cynthia's best friend, Maxine. She and her boyfriend, Ted, were watching. Ted was into fast cars and discos, as was Maxine, so they could only have been at the Grants if Cynthia had talked them into coming.

"Look, Cynthia," I said quickly, trying desperately to undo the damage, "Toby wouldn't have hurt you, but I should have remembered that you hadn't been to a horse place before, so it's really my fault. I—"

"Yes, it is your fault," Cynthia said, "and when I get home—"

"You'll make whatever trouble you can for your little sister," Alan finished. "What a sweet thought! Janet, if you run into any static you'll know who to thank."

Cynthia, white-faced, stared at him for a moment, then wheeled. "Let's get out of this stinking place," she said.

Alan looked at me. "Will what I said make things harder for you at home?" he asked. "About halfway through, it occurred to me that it might."

He walked forward and reached up to put his hand on mine, clasping the reins. "Come clean now! What's the situation at home?"

"Mom doesn't like me riding. In fact, she hates it. I bought Toby with my own money, but, of course, if she forbids me to ride and makes trouble for Mrs. Smith . . ." Suddenly and for the first time it occurred to me that Mrs. Smith could take care of herself and would be quite a match for Mother.

"I wouldn't worry about your mother throwing her weight around the Smith farm. I'll bet Aunt Jessie is more than a match for her. Funny, I'd heard your mother had this thing about riding. Wish I'd thought of it sooner. Look, if Cynthia makes trouble, will you let me know?"

"Thanks a lot, but what could you do?"

"Who knows? But my father has a certain amount of standing in the legal world."

"I didn't know he was a lawyer. I thought he just . . . well . . . farmed and rode horses."

"His main interest is the farm here, but he does have some kind of semi-partnership with a law firm downtown, and his brother-in-law—my uncle—is on the state supreme court. So, your mother might listen to them."

"How could they change her?"

"They might invite her to lunch or something and ask her to come to one of the affairs here, where she could see that the people are comparatively harmless."

"It's not that. It's just that she has this . . . this prejudice against riding. I really don't understand it. When I asked her about it she said it was because riding was a snobbish thing for rich people."

"So are a lot of things—sailing, yachts, polo and first class travel. When she travels for her firm, does she go coach or first class?"

I grinned. "First class."

"There you are. Dad always goes coach."

I had this sudden vision of Alan's father, whom I had never seen, sitting squeezed in the middle seat of a three-seat coach unit wearing his hunting pink, boots and hunting cap.

"What's so funny?" Alan said. "Share the joke."

I told him my vision of his father in hunting pink in a coach seat.

He grinned. "As a matter of fact, I can't think of anybody who'd enjoy the thought of that more than Dad. You're going to have to meet him and tell him."

"Oh no! I couldn't!"

"Why not? Don't be silly!"

"Well, I have to go in the arena now anyway. I'm late. They're doing ratings."

He waved. "I'll hunt you down later."

The rating was fascinating. Kids of all ages with their ponies stood under huge letters put up around the arena. There were D1, D2 and D3, and C1, C2 and C3, representing the various ratings, of which the lowest was D3 and the highest C1. In the arena a single rider performed dressage for a group of examiners. After the dressage, the rider dismounted and stood beside his or her horse while the examiners went over the horse and the tack, testing its flexibility or dryness and asking the rider questions. Then the next rider came in to be examined.

"There you are."

I looked back and saw Mrs. Smith coming through the door. "I've been looking for you."

"Cynthia, my sister, was here, and I've been talking to her."

"I didn't know she rode."

"She doesn't. She was . . . was just here with friends." Since Mrs. Smith was not alone I didn't feel like going into any details about her and Alan. Standing with Mrs. Smith was a tall man with chestnut hair and gray eyes.

"James, I'd like you to meet Janet West. Janet, this is my brother, James Pendleton."

"How do you do?" I said. I had to dismount anyway, so I got off, pulled the reins over Toby's head and held out my hand.

He smiled. "I do very well. What about you?"

"Fine thanks."

"My young cousin, Alan, has spoken of you."

"Oh. Are you sure he wasn't talking about my sister, Cynthia?"

"No. He spoke about Cynthia, too. Are you coming to be rated?"

"Yes." I looked at Mrs. Smith.

"Why don't you go and join that gaggle of riders there to one side," she said. "They're unrated. And I'm going to have to go, too. Gerry, one of the examiners, has to leave before long, and I'm to take her place."

"And I'm coming to watch," Mr. Pendleton said.

60

He had on riding clothes that seemed well-worn, and his face, while not exactly tan in the way people at the beach get tan, looked as though he'd been out in the sun a lot.

I stood there with the other kids and watched while the examiners told the rider being rated to walk, trot, canter, then back to trot and walk again. She had to dismount and then mount again. Then she was questioned and her horse checked and its harness examined. Eventually, my turn came. I led Toby out to where Mrs. Smith and Mr. Pendleton were standing with the other examiners.

"All right, Janet. Mount," Mrs. Smith said. "Now walk slowly around the inner ring here and then change to a trot."

I went through all the procedures that I saw the others had gone through. I walked Toby, trotted him, broke into a canter, and then back to a trot and a walk.

"Remember to keep your shoulders back and your hands lower. I know it sounds contradictory, but you're supposed to look both straight and relaxed in your seat. The only thing worse than leaning forward is leaning back. Leaning back is the sure road to falling off and also incidentally pulling at the horse's mouth. But leaning forward is ungraceful and it makes you too inclined to pull on the rein. Now dismount and bring Toby over here. I want to ask you some questions."

The questions concerned Toby's care—how to feed him, groom him, how to keep his tack clean and flexible, and how to cool him when he had been out.

"How long have you been riding, Janet?" Mr. Pendleton said, coming over to look at Toby.

"A little over a year. Alan Grant says Toby's a good horse. I think he's wonderful." Maybe, I thought, it was Cynthia's comment that made me so anxious for him to appreciate Toby.

"Alan's right. He is. How much did you pay for him?"

"Four hundred dollars."

"You got a very good buy indeed. You're both lucky." He smiled, and I could feel myself blushing. Maybe he was a poor father for Judy. But he sounded great to me.

"Did your mother give him to you for birthday or Christmas?"

"No," I said. "I bought him myself." Something made me add, "I earned the money."

He smiled. "How?"

"Babysitting."

"I take off my hat to you."

"Thank you."

I got back on Toby and rode back to where the others were gathered.

CHAPTER 8

I was given a C1 rating, which set me up no end. I had been sure I wouldn't get anything better than a D.

"Congratulations," Mrs. Smith said as we were driving back in the trailer. "Considering that's your first rating and the fact that you haven't had any real coaching, it's excellent." She grinned. "Shows you I was right about your being a natural rider. James wanted me to put you even higher, but then he's taken a shine to you."

"I think he's terrific. And I can't understand why—" I stopped, embarrassed.

"Were you going to say you couldn't understand why Judy has such a poor opinion of him?"

I looked quickly at her. "You know, then."

"Everybody knows. She's not exactly reticent with her opinion, but then she's hardly objective. She's been brought up to believe that her father was the monster of all time. Which, I am bound to say, was not too far off when he was careening around the countryside getting drunk and crashing cars and chasing girls. It was around then that Judy's mother left him, and she's had complete custody of Judy until now. And, of course, Judy's mad that she can't go abroad with her mother."

"So she takes it out on her father?"

She smiled. "Emotions are rarely logical."

"I know," I said. And my mind went to riding and Mother's attitude towards it. Then I remembered Alan's conversation with Cynthia, and my spirits, which had been high, plummeted. Wearily, I took off my jumping cap.

"Mrs. Smith," I blurted out, "Mother . . . Mother may be upset about something that happened this afternoon."

She looked surprised. "Was she there? I didn't see her."

"No, but Cynthia, my sister, was. She . . . she has sort of a crush on Alan, and I think she got her friend, Maxine, to drive her there to see him." And I repeated the exchange that had taken place among Cynthia, Alan and me. "Alan said afterwards that he might have got me in trouble at home and was sorry."

"So he ought to have been." Mrs. Smith hesitated. "When he comes to help out with things like the Pony Club rally, he can be wonderful. But he has the kind of arrogance that seems to afflict most of the males of our family. I suppose it comes from their all being so good-looking. Women from nine to ninety show a tendency to make fools of themselves over them. I could tell you tales about James, my brother, in his wild oats days. . . ." She sighed. "But I guess I won't. It's water under the bridge, anyway. And the sad part of it all is that the females of the family suffer from chronic insecurity. Probably one springs from the other."

I thought about Mia and her anger and defiance. "Is that what's the matter with Mia? I mean, I know you said that it was because you tried to make her interested in riding . . ." I hesitated, deciding, belatedly, that that wasn't the most tactful thing I could have said.

"In a way." We drove for a few minutes in silence. Then Mrs. Smith went on. "James, my brother, rode effortlessly from the time he first mounted a horse at the age of six. I began later and it was hard work for me. I determined this wouldn't be true for Mia. So, I started her riding almost before she could walk, thinking to do her a favor. Instead of which she felt I was forcing it on her, and consequently blames me for the accident, which is much easier to do than make herself climb back on again. It's all very ironic."

"Wouldn't it be better to send her to a school which has never seen a horse?"

"Yes. But I'd also like one that has never seen a drug. And it's not that easy to find—especially for a girl with a poor to lousy academic rating. And such a school, if and when you find it, is usually pretty strict—not to say old-fashioned. Even horseless, it'd be anathema to Mia."

"It's funny," I said slowly. "Do you think people who hate something are afraid of it?"

"Yes, one way or another. Why? What are you thinking?"

"About Mother, and the way she hates me riding."

"Did she ever ride?"

"No—or least I don't think so."

We were silent again for a while. Then Mrs. Smith said, "It might be something even she herself is not aware of."

"I guess so."

"But in the meantime that's not helping you with what you may find at home, is it?"

"I suppose I'll just have to handle it when I get there."

"All right. But let me know if I can help."

I settled Toby in his stall, brushing him and giving him food and water. Then, when his nose started nuzzling around my pockets, I let him have the carrot he knew was in each. "You're terrific!" I said to him and planted a kiss in the middle of his forehead. Then I biked home, trying desperately not to entertain the thought that that might be the last time I saw him. But the nearer I got to home, the more I felt doom hanging over Toby and me. It was six-thirty by the time I reached the house, later than I thought I would be. There was nobody in the kitchen, so I sneaked upstairs to take off my riding clothes and have a shower. I was pretty sure Mother was making it up when she talked about smelling the stable when she came into my room, but I wasn't going to take any chances.

I was in the shower in the bathroom Cynthia and I share when Mother banged on the door.

"Janet? Are you in there?"

I turned down the water. "Yes, Mom. Do you want me for something?" I could feel my heart beating.

"Yes. I want to talk to you. Come down as soon as you're dressed."

The word "talk" had an ominous ring. Earlier in the week we had had a "talk" about my irresponsible behavior in forgetting my babysitting commitment to the Turners.

"You simply don't tell somebody you're going to do something, let them count on it, and then not show," Mother had said bitingly.

"I'm sorry," I said. "I've already apologized to Mrs. Turner."

I debated adding that it was an accident and that I hadn't done such a thing before. Luckily, before the words came out, I realized that they would provide a perfect opportunity for Mother to dwell on her favorite theme: that Toby was occupying far too much of my time and attention. So I just lowered my eyes in what I hope looked like remorse and slid out. As a matter of fact, I was sorry and had said so to Mrs. Turner.

66

Mother was fixing dinner when I came down after my shower. She glanced up from the stove when I came in.

"What happened this afternoon, Janet?" she asked. "Cynthia came back saying she'd been insulted by Alan and that you joined in with him." She turned the flame under the pan low, put a lid on it, and turned around, leaning against the oven door with her arms crossed.

I could feel my heart pounding—beat, beat, beat.

I took a breath. "Alan needled Cynthia because she was needling me, saying put-down things about Toby, saying no matter what I paid for him it was too much. And she did that because when she walked up behind him, he wheeled and stamped. Alan told her that before she came to a pony rally, she ought to learn never to come up behind a horse, and he said that what she said about Toby proved she didn't know anything, that he was a good horse." I took another breath. It was like taking a jump, only worse. But the jump had to be taken. "And you know, Mom, I'm sick to death of feeling scared every time I come home that you're going to make me stop riding. You don't beat on Cynthia the way you do me. I told . . . I told somebody today that you don't like me. You never have. I didn't know it until I said that. But I know now, it's true. You don't." I stood there, waiting for the ceiling to fall in.

Mother went absolutely white. "That is not true! I don't play favorites."

"Yes, you do. Even Cynthia said you did, remember? Well I'm going to tell you something. One of these days I'm going to be old enough to be free. I'm going to find out how old I have to be before I can live on my own. I'm sick of the way you treat me."

And I turned and walked out of the house.

I didn't have my handbag with me, which meant I didn't have any money. But I did have my bike, which was parked in the garage, so I went and got it and wheeled it out to the sidewalk. I thought I heard Mother calling as I set off down the street, but I kept going.

What I wanted to do was go straight back to the barn, so I could be with Toby and with Mrs. Smith. But as I biked around the neighborhood I couldn't help feeling that that might be the worst thing I could do—that Mother would use it as an excuse to keep me away from Mrs. Smith and the farm. I thought also about her brother, James Pendleton, and how kind he had been and how she had said he'd "taken a shine to me."

Thinking about him, I decided to go to the stable anyway and turned the bike around. But after I'd covered a hundred yards or so, I thought again about how Mother would react if she discovered I was there. It would probably be the final straw against Toby. So once more I turned my bike and, not having any other creative ideas, wheeled it in the general direction of the nearby shopping mall. I still didn't have any money, but the mall wasn't far from school, and I might run into somebody I could borrow a dollar from. I hated borrowing money and was furious at myself for leaving money upstairs. But then I hadn't known I was going to walk out.

It was dark by the time I got to the mall. I didn't dare park my bicycle, because although there was a place where it could be stashed safely, to lock it in would cost a quarter. So I walked along the mall, wheeling my bike and looking in the windows, wondering what to do next.

The more I walked, the more I smelled the aroma of hamburger, which was coming from the burger shop at the end of the mall. Since I wasn't hungry and didn't have any money anyway, it was dumb to keep on going, but I did, anyway. When I got there I stared in the window. A bunch of kids from school were sitting around in the booths and at the tables. What surprised me a lot, though, was to see Morris Blair behind the counter, serving up the burgers as they were passed through from the kitchen. Seeing him gave me a guilty pang as I remembered that I had walked out on him and his mother last weekend. As I was standing there, wondering whether I should go and speak to him, he looked up, put his hand over his eyes to blot out the light, and stared towards me. Then he wiped his hands, pushed up a piece of the counter, and came out into the main part of the shop. I waved at him. He opened the door and came out. "Hi," he said.

"Hi! I'm sorry I left so abruptly last Sunday."

"Yeah. Ma didn't know what she'd said. Why did you?"

"I guess because she asked about Cynthia."

"So what's wrong with that?"

"Nothing. I'm sorry, Morris. I guess . . . There've been an awful lot of people who thought the only thing about me that was important at all was that I was Cynthia's sister. I was rude. I'll write your mother a letter."

"You don't have to do that. Just call her up. Here, here's our number." He got out his pad and scribbled a number. I took it. I seemed to be in trouble with everybody.

"What's the matter?" Morris asked.

I stood there, holding my bicycle, not saying anything, but feeling as though something building up inside were going to burst.

"Come on," Morris said. And he put his hand on my shoulder and shook it.

"I've run away from home. Mother doesn't like me. Cynthia is mad at me because Alan insulted her, and I'm always terrified that she's going to make me give up Toby."

"Toby, your horse?"

"Yes. And he's more important to me than anybody else."

"Maybe that's the reason your mother wants to take him away. I mean, after all, I guess she thinks she ought to come before a horse."

"You don't understand," I said angrily. "I don't know why I'm telling you this. I told you, she doesn't like me." And then I burst into tears.

"Here," Morris said after a moment. He thrust something into my hand, and I saw it was a paper napkin. "It's clean," he said. "I just got it from the dispenser."

I mopped and cried and mopped and cried.

"I didn't mean not to be understanding," he said after a minute. "It must be tough to feel your mother doesn't like you. Are you sure about it?"

I blew my nose. "Well she hasn't said so, if that's what you mean. But she holds Toby over my head every time I do anything that she doesn't like or doesn't approve of. Even Cynthia told her she was unfair. But Cynthia's mad at me now, too."

"Because of what Alan said to her? What did he say, by the way?"

I told him the whole thing about Cynthia's being at the Pony Club and about her coming up behind Toby and everything that was said after that between her and Alan.

"He sure didn't make it easier for you," Morris said now. "He's quite bright, but he's inclined to show off."

"How do you know he's quite bright?" I said. "You're in my class, not his."

"I do math and science in his class."

"Oh, yes, I'd forgotten. You mean he's quite bright at those subjects?"

"He could be a lot brighter, if he worked. But he's not that interested."

"What's he interested in?"

"Girls." Morris said it simply, then seeing me looking up at him, grinned. "On a full-time basis. I'd say next to that he's probably interested in horses, like you are, but I think he likes to get girls interested in him. Once they are, he can be very uninterested in them. It's a thing with him."

"Maybe that's why he's acting towards Cynthia the way he does now."

"Probably. And the more she shows she likes him, the more he'll put her down. I know you say you two aren't speaking, but somebody ought to tell her that."

"That sounds pretty rotten, I mean, really gross. And it's not as though he has to make up for not being good looking or something, because he really is."

"Don't tell me you're afflicted like Cynthia," Morris said. "Hey!" He put out his hand and took my arm. "You're not, are you?"

"No, but what difference does it make to you?" The moment I asked that, I realized everything it implied, and I could feel the blush coming up from my toes. "Not that it's any of my business," I added hastily.

"It makes a difference to me because I like you. I like you a lot better than I like any other girl in school."

There was a silence. I couldn't see in the dark whether Morris was blushing or not, but I was. I didn't mean to say what I said at that moment, but it fell out. "I wish you liked riding, it'd be really neat!"

"Well I don't. Or rather, I don't mind it. I've ridden out west. But I don't have the time or money now. I have to have a job as well as school, to help with college. So something has to give and it's riding. If that's the condition for your liking me, then I'll have to live without it."

"Morris, I didn't mean it that way. I do like you. I like you a lot."

"That's neat. I mean it's great!" He reached out and took my hand.

At that point the door opened and a man looked out. "Hey, Morris! People are lining up for eats. Have you decided to abandon the working life?"

"No," Morris said. "I'm coming back." He said to me. "Come on in and have some coffee at the counter or something. I get off in half an hour when the other guy comes in. We're going to have to decide what you're going to do about going back."

"If I go back, Mother'll just say I have to sell Toby and what an awful person I am."

"Maybe not. Come in. We'll talk about it."

CHAPTER 9

"You're going to have to go home, because what else can you do? In the first place, you don't have any money to live anywhere else, do you?"

I shook my head.

"And in the second place, do you really want to run away on a permanent basis?"

I stirred my coffee. I was sitting at the counter. Morris had taken a half dozen orders when he came back, thrust some coffee at me, and worked hard for a while filling orders and waiting on the tables. Finally, the rush had died down, and he'd come back to talk to me. "By the way, have you had any dinner?"

"No. I'm not hungry."

"Do you lose your appetite when you get upset?"

"Yes."

"Well, it's dumb not to eat, so I'll give you a tunafish sandwich. That's pretty digestible. Or would you rather have cheese?"

"I'd like to have a tuna melt," I said, and realized that my appetite had returned. "But I don't have any money. I came out without my bag."

"I'll lend it to you.' As he started to fix the sandwich, the manager came back. "Everything all right?" he asked, looking at me.

"Absolutely." I decided that I'd better put in a

word to help Morris. "I wasn't going to have anything to eat, but Morris talked me into it."

"Adda boy!" the manager said. "Just don't keep him so distracted that he doesn't serve any of the other customers."

This time I saw Morris blush. It was true that his ears stuck out some, but he was really quite good looking. What's more, he was bright-looking. I decided that that was important.

"Here's your melt," he said. "Want a soda?"

"Well—" I was still thinking of my lack of money.

"What kind?"

"Coke."

"Coming up."

"So you think I'd better go home."

"Yes, go home and negotiate."

"Is that what you do with your mother—negotiate?"

"Sort of. If she finds I really don't want to do something she thinks I ought to do, we at least talk about it. I'll say this about her, she doesn't push her weight around. She lets me be myself."

I thought about Mother. Ever since I'd had Toby I'd been so crazy about him that I didn't bother to look back at what life at home had been like before his arrival, but I did now. Was it better?

Yes. It was. But not completely. There was the matter of our bedroom when Cynthia and I shared it. Of the two I was the messier, but it was also true that when Mother came into the room, she didn't even stop to find out whose things were on the floor or all over the bureau. She'd just lay into me.

"You know," I said now. "It isn't just Toby. Mom was always like that—always criticizing me more than Cynthia."

"Have you told her that? I mean, more than just getting mad about Cynthia."

"If you mean, have I sat down and talked to her about it, no. Not really. I don't really know why I didn't before I got Toby. But since then, I've always thought that the lower I kept my head the better."

Morris poured himself some coffee. "You're still going to have to talk to her. You're just not old enough to go it alone."

"Kids do," I grumbled. "We read about them all the time. They just disappear."

"And what happens then to Toby?"

I stared down into my soda. "I guess you're right." I sighed. "I'd better go home now before it gets any worse."

"If you wait five minutes, I'll go with you. Here comes Chris now. I'll be with you in a sec, as soon as I fill him in on what's in operation."

Chris Temple, a slightly older boy than Morris walked in, pushed up the counter and went behind it. "How's business?" he asked casually.

"Okay. Here are some orders working. I've put down on the slips who they belong to. Come on Jan, we'll get moving."

When we got to the house I unclenched my hands and felt that they were wet.

"You're really nervous, aren't you?" Morris said after a moment.

"Yes."

"Sometimes when I'm scared I ask myself, what's the worst so and so can do?"

"She can make me sell Toby. That's the worst, and I worry about it all the time."

"If Toby is legally yours, how can she do that?"

"She can call up Mrs. Smith and tell her she doesn't

want me to spend time mucking out stables. If I don't do that, then I can't keep him in the barn."

"Do you really think she'd do that?"

"Yes," I said. My voice shook. I could feel the tears behind my throat. I'd cried once in front of Morris. I didn't want to do it again. "I'd better go in."

"I'll go with you."

I wheeled my bike into the garage. Then, deciding against going in the kitchen door, I went to the front door and rang the bell. The door opened. Mother stood there.

She looked as white as she had before and just as angry. Cynthia, behind her, looked scared. Then, as Morris appeared behind me, Mother's expression changed.

"You're Morris Blair, aren't you?" she said.

"Yes, Mrs. West."

"Normally I'd be delighted to invite you in, but right now I have to have a conference with Janet."

"Thanks, but I couldn't stay anyway. You'd have been proud of her today, Mrs. West. She rode beautifully."

Mother's brows went up. "Were you there? I didn't know you rode."

There was a tiny silence, and, as though she were saying them now, I heard Mother's voice repeating the words, "Mrs. Blair is really a very good secretary." Then Cynthia gave a small, quickly stifled giggle.

"I rode some out West," Morris said. "I haven't done it here, but I heard some of the kids talking."

"I see." Mother said.

I didn't see, because if that were true, how come Morris hadn't told me earlier? But I decided not to question it now. "Well," I said, turning to Morris, "thanks for bringing me home. I'll see you at school."

After the door closed behind Morris, I stayed there in the hall, knowing a storm was coming, and feeling that I might as well face it immediately. "What was it you wanted to talk to me about, Mom?"

"About those terrible things you accused me of, before walking out. How dare you—?"

Where I got the courage I don't know, unless it had been grafted on me from Morris when he was bringing me home. "What do you mean, 'how dare I' like I had no right to say what I think? I'm tired of being always in the wrong. I have a right to ride, it's my horse, I paid for him, and I'm paying for his lessons." Suddenly I remembered Morris's word, "negotiate." I wasn't doing much negotiating. "Can't we arrive at some kind of agreement?" I said.

"The agreement that would please me most would be the one where you sold your wretched horse and took an interest in something healthier. But I'm not going to force you." She took a deep breath. "If I was unfair to you this afternoon, when I accused you of helping Alan Grant put Cynthia down, I'm sorry."

Cynthia and I stared at each other. Then she said, "Alan Grant is some kind of creepy snob."

"Even though he's Romeo?"

"Especially because he's Romeo. Why should I care what he says?" And she flounced up stairs. Mother stared down at her hands.

"Do I really treat the two of you that differently?" she asked in an queer, hesitant voice.

"Well, Mom, don't you listen to yourself? Don't you hear it? Sometimes I wonder . . . I mean is there a reason you do this, besides just liking Cynthia better? Did I do something at an early age that kind of turned you against me? I know I'm not as pretty and not as clever—"

That was as far as I got. Mother suddenly folded me in a bear hug, and after a minute I realized she was crying, too.

"I'm sorry, I'm sorry," she said. "I still don't like your riding. But—things'll be better, I promise you. Now go to bed, before I have an old-fashioned case of hysterics!" She kissed me, thrust me away, and went off towards the kitchen.

Slowly I went upstairs. Outside Cynthia's door I hesitated, wondering if there was something I could say to make peace. But while I was standing there she opened the door. "Yes?" she said. "You want something?"

"No, not especially. I'm . . . I'm sorry things didn't seem to work out this afternoon . . ." I heard my words, hating myself for my pussyfooting attitude. I wasn't pussyfooting with Mother. I faced her. Why was I tiptoeing around Cynthia? But I still couldn't think of anything helpful to say.

That night, lying in bed, I kept thinking about what Mother had said, and how she promised things would be better. I wanted to believe her but somehow I couldn't.

"How were things at home last night?" Mrs. Smith asked when I arrived at the barn the next afternoon. I was going to coach Mia for an hour or so, then clean out Toby's stall and exercise him.

"Not great," I said. "Though I guess they could have been worse. At least Mother isn't threatening to make me sell Toby." I paused. "She said she was sorry, and that she didn't mean to play favorites. And that she won't try to stop me riding."

"I've been thinking about that. As a matter of fact, my brother James and I were talking about it at dinner. To ease your mind, if the worse should happen, he'll buy Toby on a temporary basis. When things ease up a bit—

and I'm sure they will—you can buy him back. In the meantime you can come out and exercise him."

She and I looked at each other for a moment. "Short of locking you in your room," she said, "I don't think your mother can prevent you from coming here if you want to."

"Wouldn't she be able to force me—maybe in court?"

"Technically, she might. But I don't think she'll put it to the test. She would look very silly taking you to court, or taking me to court, over your wanting to ride your horse."

It was like half a load coming off my back. The other half—the knowledge of how much Mother disliked me being at the barn and having Toby—remained. But the fear that she would do something to take him away lessened.

Mrs. Smith smiled. "Run along and see what you can do with Mia," she said, "then come back and I'll give you a lesson."

Mia scowled when I walked into her study room. "I hear you're the hot new favorite," she said. "Ma and Uncle James spent the whole dinnertime talking about you."

I sat down on the chair beside the table. "You know, we really should change places. You sound like me talking to my mother." I hesitated for a moment or so, then said, "Want to study some English?"

"What'll it get me?"

"Maybe entrance to a school that you and your mother both like."

"That'll be the day."

"Come on, it can't hurt you."

She seemed to hesitate, then shrugged and came back to the table. "For today."

We worked for about an hour. I'd learned that if I could get Mia interested, she did well, and she learned quickly. "That's not the kind of sonnet you were talking about last time," she said pugnaciously at some point.

"No, it's a different kind. The rhyming scheme is different." And I went on to talk about which poet used which rhyming scheme when. We finally came to a stop at the end of about an hour and a half. "I'm going to leave this book with you," I said. "It'll tell you a little about the poets, more than your book does."

I was going to the door when Mia said suddenly, "You always say we should change mothers. I'd like to meet yours. Maybe she'd like me as much as Ma likes you. And I wouldn't have to fight her about riding."

For a moment I hesitated, feeling guilty maybe about Mrs. Smith's attention to me. Then I said, "Okay, come to dinner. You can come back with me some evening when I've been here. I'll ask Mom when it'll be convenient and let you know."

"I accept," Mia said. "It'll be a great relief to get away from the barn and with somebody who feels the way I do about horses."

CHAPTER 10

"A penny for them!" James Pendleton said and smiled. When he smiled he looked less severe.

We were on a cross country ride with Mrs. Smith and a couple of other kids, and he and I seemed to be riding together.

"Nothing important." I was confused and embarrassed. What I had been thinking was not exactly what I could tell him.

"When people say that it's often because they can't—or don't want to—talk about what's in their minds." He glanced at me. "Which is it?"

Toby shied a little at that point as a squirrel suddenly tore across the road. "Whoa, Toby!" I said. "It's only a squirrel. Nothing to be afraid of." I talked and soothed Toby keeping a firm rein. After a few seconds he calmed down and went back to his trot.

"You handled that well," Mr. Pendleton said. "I can see why my sister thinks you have natural ability." He paused. "I take it your family isn't too keen on your riding."

I made a face. "That's putting it mildly. Mother hates it, but I guess we've reached some sort of . . . of"—agreement didn't seem quite the right word—"of . . ."

"Accord?" He asked.

"I suppose so."

"Has she ever told you why she dislikes your riding so much?"

"She says it's snobbish, that horsey people are all snobs."

He winced a little. "Ouch!" he said, "Is that your experience?"

"No. Of course, I haven't really had much to do with some of the bigger farms. Maybe she's right about those. But it isn't true about Mrs. Smith or the people I met here."

"What about your father?"

"He died when I was four."

"So you don't remember him."

"No." I paused. "Mom talks about him some. But it's hard sometimes to imagine . . ." I was about to say to imagine having a father, except that it would be such a lie. I imagined it all the time. But it wasn't real.

"What's hard to imagine?"

"What he was like," I finished limply. There was no way I was going to talk about my fantasy father, who was always on my side and who thought I was wonderful—sort of like Fantasy George. At that point, thinking about George, I giggled.

"It's against the law to giggle at something without sharing it, so what is it?"

I had never talked about Fantasy George, but then I'd never met anyone—or at least any adult—as sympathetic as James Pendleton. Still I hesitated, surprised that I would be confiding in him like this. Finally I said, "You'll laugh!"

"Maybe. But with you, not at you."

"Well, I have this imaginary friend called George. He's always ready to knock people down when they hassle me."

82

"He sounds wonderful, if a little warlike. I had a friend like that, once, only she was a girl named Nancy. At a time when I thought I was the ugliest human being God ever made, she would tell me how handsome I was. Is George a little like that?"

"Yes." I glanced quickly at him as we turned the horses up a trail. "It's hard to imagine you thinking you were ugly."

"It's hard to imagine you needing somebody to reassure you about being loved and protected and attractive." He looked at me and smiled. "But isn't that George's basic function, I mean besides knocking people down."

I giggled again. "Yes."

We rode for a while as the path climbed up a hill and down into a field. I felt strange having this conversation with a man. The only men I'd ever talked to were teachers and the family dentist and doctor, and that didn't count, because we talked about studies or teeth or bodies, not about feelings. As a matter of fact, I thought, steering Toby around a rabbit hole, I hadn't much talked to anyone—except Toby, of course—about how I felt, except when I was angry—especially angry about Toby.

"Mr. Pendleton," I said suddenly, "why is it so much easier to talk about feelings when you're angry than when you're feeling something else?"

"Pendleton is such a long name. Why don't you call me James, the way everybody else does?" He turned and smiled at me.

I could feel a blush of pleasure. "Won't it be funny calling you James but calling Mrs. Smith 'Mrs. Smith?'"

"Maybe. But what you call my sister doesn't really have that much to do with what you call me. Besides, Smith is a much more callable name than Pendleton, which has at least two too many syllables." He paused.

"Back to your question, though. Feelings that are pushed forward by a rush of energy are always much easier to express. In fact, it's hard not to express them. Self-control was a highly prized quality in my generation—much more so than in yours. So that not saying the angry word was always considered a virtue. What was that line? 'If you can fill the unforgiving minute with sixty second's worth of distance run,' et cetera."

" 'If,' " I said. "Kipling. Most of the kids in class sort of laughed at it, but I liked it."

"It's considered passé now, but one of these days somebody's going to rediscover it, and then it will be admired again."

We trotted along and then as we came to an open trail, cantered. Mr. Pendleton's horse was a tall chestnut named Border Boy. From the beginning he had seemed skittish and nervous.

"What's the matter with Border Boy?" I asked.

"He's had bad experiences and every now and then something makes him remember them. Curiously, he seems happier with narrow, closed in trails than with open ones."

"Is he yours?"

"He is now. I brought him East from California."

"Who did he belong to?"

"My former wife, but she didn't cause his skittishness. He was that way when she got him. She tried to cure him—and she handles horses well, but I don't think she really had a chance before she had to leave for London. So I bought him to carry on the good work." He leaned forward and patted the big horse on the neck.

His mention of his wife made me think of Judy and her comments about her father. "Judy hasn't been living with you, has she?"

"We haven't lived together most of her life." He

paused. "As you probably know, she isn't my greatest admirer, which makes it rough going on us both. By the way," he said, "speaking of difficult offspring, how is Mia doing?"

"Fine—I mean much better than I expected. Not that she isn't bright. The first time I saw her I thought she'd refuse to do anything. But she hasn't."

"My sister thinks she has you to thank for that, and she's grateful." He smiled at me and was about to go on when Border Boy took exception to a strangely shaped rock, "Easy boy, easy," he said, as the big horse danced and backed.

I watched his handling of Border Boy. He had a wonderful combination of gentleness and firmness. Well, I thought, he'd need it with Judy. And I felt a short, sharp jab of envy.

"Okay, you guys," Mrs. Smith called out. "Stop loitering!" She and Aldebaran were standing at the opening in the trees that led to a field. "We're going to cross the field here and get into the wide trail where we can enjoy a gallop. There are both a fence and an open path leading to the trail. Janet and Burt, I want you to take the path. Sue, Ted and I will jump the fence. James, you can do as you like, not that you wouldn't, anyway."

"Quite so," her brother replied. He started heading Border Boy towards the tall fence that lay across the pasture. Toby's ears quivered forward, and he showed signs of wanting to follow.

"Watch your horse, Janet," Mrs. Smith said. "He looks like he might like to try that jump, but you're not ready for it yet."

So Toby and I watched from across the pasture as Border Boy and his rider took the fence in a soaring leap.

"No, Toby," I said regretfully, holding onto him

when he showed signs of wanting to follow. I turned his head towards the path and then watched as Mrs. Smith, Ted and Sue also took the high fence. Of them all, I thought, even including his sister, James Pendleton jumped the best, showing the least amount of air between his seat and the saddle. One day soon, I swore to myself, I, too, would jump like that.

That evening, as I was helping Mother with the dinner, I asked her, "Can I bring Mia home for dinner one night this week?"

"Mia who?"

"Mia Smith. You know, I'm coaching her in French and English . . ." I was about to finish, ". . . to help pay for my riding lessons." But I decided to leave that alone.

"You mean the daughter of the woman who owns that stable?"

"Yes."

"Well, of course. I hope you two don't sit and talk horses all night, but other than that I'd be happy to meet her."

"She hates horses as much as you do. That's why I invited her. She said she'd like to meet you. She once agreed that we ought to switch mothers."

Mother, who was fixing some spaghetti sauce in a pot, looked up at me. "As bad as that, is it?"

"I didn't mean it was bad," I said hastily.

"By all means bring her," Mother said. "It ought to be interesting."

Mia came home with me three days later, both of us being driven by one of the barn girls. My bike was in the back of the car, and I told Mrs. Smith that Mother or Cynthia would drive Mia back.

"I hear you don't like horses," Mother said to Mia as we sat down to dinner.

"Hate them," Mia said, "oversized, unintelligent beasts."

I couldn't let that pass. "Toby has lots of intelligence. You don't have to run them down just because you don't like them."

"Then it wasn't very bright of you to invite her, was it?" Cynthia said with her serpent's smile. "You brought Mia home because she and Mom have this common bond, so you can't expect them not to talk about it."

"I still don't think that's an excuse to make Janet think we're picking on her," Mother said and gave me a smile. "There are lots of other things we can talk about."

"I'd like to hear about taking law," Mia said. "I've been thinking about that as one of the things I might go in for—that is, if I can get to a decent school."

"What school are you trying for?"

"Well . . ." Mia looked at me for a moment. "The one I'd like to go to is Broadhurst, but Ma seems to think it's too near New York and is full of druggies."

"I hear it's a good school," Mother said, "though not as good as it used to be, and for the reason your mother says. It has a new head now, and they seem to have got through that bad patch. But there are other schools, more or less of the same type and quality, that haven't had troubles like that, or if they have, have handled them well. A couple of the lawyers in my firm went to one of them. I can get their names for you."

"That'd be great, Mrs. West. Thanks!"

"Where does your mother want you to go?"

Mia mentioned the name of a horsey school in Virginia. "Mother went there, and of course I can get in even though my grades are lousy."

"Don't be too sure," Mother surprised me by saying. "A lot of those schools that seemed to specialize in rich, not very bright girls are changing their ways. Some of them are getting quite choosy about the scholastic aptitude of some of the girls whom they would once have taken, no questions asked."

"Well, maybe I just won't go to school at all . . . unless Janet can get me good grades in entrance exams."

"No coach can get you in, only you can do that. All Janet can do is to tell you what to do yourself. Then you have to do it. Is she being a help?"

"Yes, when I let her," Mia said with great honesty. "But I think that Ma—Mother—likes her so much and thinks she's such a good rider that she'd teach her anyway, even if I don't pass all those exams."

I was pleased and flattered and embarrassed and stole a look at Mother to see if she was impressed.

"Janet's good at a lot of things beside riding," Mother said. "And I hope, when she gets over this phase, she'll put her energy into something a little more productive."

"Like wanting to be a lawyer?" Mia asked.

"Yes," Mother replied. "Or a doctor or a writer or a business executive—whatever she chooses to be."

Mia looked at her over her forkful of spaghetti, but didn't say anything. Mother then asked Cynthia about the play, and the conversation stayed on that for the rest of the dinner.

Afterwards, when Mia and I were up in my room talking and listening to some records, I said, "Still want us to switch mothers?"

"I'll tell you about mothers. There's a law, like Murphy's law. Whatever you are or want to be, your mother wants you to be something else."

"It's not true of Cynthia," I said gloomily.

"Yeah, well, she looks like your mother and sounds like her when she talks—her voice, I mean—so your mom probably sees her as reliving her own life. You're the oddball."

I couldn't argue about it, and, after all, I'd invited Mia here because our mothers seemed to want the opposite for us, but I suddenly decided that the whole thing was a bad idea, although I wasn't quite sure why. Mother had surprised me by sticking up for me at dinner, but in the end it had been the old story: without being particularly nice to Mia she'd managed to get across her message—riding is stupid.

And of course Cynthia was being bitchy as she had been so much lately. In fact, it was hard to remember that sometimes she'd been nice, but not since that day at the rally when she saw Alan.

What's worse than a girl in love
With a boy in love
With somebody else?

. . . I sang to myself later as I went up to bed. But it wasn't really true. Alan was not in love, to my knowledge, with anyone else.

CHAPTER 11

Toby remained his wonderful self and the most important person in my life. A vet I once knew said that cats and horses were alike in that they knew who liked them and acted accordingly. Most dogs, on the other hand, were born assuming the world loved them and loved the world back.

Toby ignored the other barn grooms who, on the rare days I couldn't be there, cleaned out his stall and took him out. One of the girls swore that he curled his upper lip at her, in the manner of an old-fashioned aristocrat. But he nickered and whinnied the moment I entered the barn area and liked to rub his head up and down my front and blow gently, and then search in my pockets for goodies.

> *King Toby the Splendid*
> *With virtue appended*
> *And foes all up ended*
> *To his court he attended*
> *And granted each plea . . .*

. . . I sang one day as I groomed him. Not perhaps the greatest ode in the English language, I thought, bringing the brush down Toby's side. Nevertheless, I was quite pleased with it.

"Stunning lyrics," a voice said from the back of the stall.

I turned. "Oh hello, Alan. Yes, Toby likes them and they were composed especially for him. Don't you, Toby?" And I planted a kiss on his forehead.

"You're going to give that animal ideas above his station, Alan said. "Why don't you practice on me instead?"

"Funny man," I replied and put the brushes back on the shelf. "What are you doing here now, anyway? There isn't a pony rally."

"I came to help the fair Jessica get up the questions for the next rating day. Should I practice them on you first?"

"Well, if I'm going to be rated, probably not."

"How honorable you are. Depressingly so. Why can't you be like other girls?"

"What other girls?" I asked suspiciously.

"Well, for example, your sister."

I was furious at Cynthia, but that didn't mean I was going to criticize her with Alan. "That's a gross and tacky thing to say, Alan Grant. I'm surprised at you." Which I wasn't, of course. It was just the kind of thing Alan would do.

"I stand reproved. In that case, let's go for a ride."

"I thought you were supposed to be helping Mrs. Smith with the rating questions."

"I am, but not until five. I was going to exercise Mahatma anyway. He needs more than just riding over here."

"All right," I said. "Let me get Toby's saddle on." I had been grooming him in an open area while he was between crossties. I turned to go for his saddle.

"What I like about you is your enthusiasm," Alan said. "It does worlds for a guy's ego."

I came back with the saddle. "Alan, your ego doesn't need building up."

"How do you know I'm not one mass of quivering sensitivity?"

I pulled Toby's girth strap firm. "How do I know that Toby isn't a Thoroughbred stallion? Don't you try your soft soap on me, Alan. It won't work. I know you're only interested in girls who aren't interested in you, and then when you sweet talk them into being interested, you leave them flat. That's rotten."

"Don't be such a moralist! And anyway, there are girls who only chase boys who aren't interested and treat them exactly the same. It's not a purely male characteristic."

I mounted. "I never said it was. Okay, let's go. Where's your horse?"

Mahatma turned out to be a black hunter that looked about twice as big as Toby. "Why did you call him Mahatma? I thought he'd be small and Arabian or Persian looking."

"I didn't name him. He was already named, but I think the name suits him. He has a peaceful look though determined nature."

We rode away from the national park this time, through some pastures and down to a lake. There was a trail running alongside the lake where we could canter and even gallop. After a while we left the horses where they could graze and sat by the lake and threw pebbles into it.

"Your mother any more reconciled to your becoming an Olympic equestrian?"

"Ha ha," I said. Then I sighed. "No, I'm afraid not. She seems to be permanently anti-horse."

Alan lay down on the grass and stared at the sky. "Ever asked her why?"

"Lots of times."

"What does she say?"

"What I already told you: that riding is a snobbish upper-crust activity. And she goes on thinking that even though she does travel first class. But of course that's because she travels for the company."

"And I notice that she works with one of the snootier of the law offices in town, not for legal aid or in the public defender's office or anything like that."

"It may have something to do with the fact that she has to support two daughters."

"True. By the way, I spoke to Dad, and he got moving on some kind of high-toned lawyer's lunch next week and suggested to one of the partners in Mrs. West's law firm that he might bring her along."

"Thanks," I said. Privately, I didn't think it would have the slightest effect on Mother's view of riding. The fact that Mr. Grant, a lawyer, spent more of his time on a horse than in a legal office and was the local Master of Hounds wouldn't move Mother at all. She'd just think he was stupid. However, I saw no point in telling Alan that. But I did say before I could think of its implications, "You know, if you really want to help me you'd be nice to Cynthia." Then I realized that it was practically telling Alan that she was moping around for him.

"I mean . . ." I said hastily and then was stuck. There was really no way I could fix that. And if Cynthia ever heard about it, she'd do everything she could to feed Mother's dislike of Toby. "Look, please, please don't tell anyone I said that, because if you tell anyone, anyone at all, it'll get back to Cynthia."

"And then she'd fix Toby for good, wouldn't she?" He sat up on one elbow and looked at me.

"Yes. She's not always like that. Sometimes—well, once lately—she's seemed nice and supportive. But not if she heard that I'd said what I did. So please promise, won't you?"

Alan gave an elaborate and theatrical sigh and lay down again. "I was thinking it was a dandy thing I could hold over your head." Then he put his hand to his forehead. "I implore you, for Toby's sake, Janet, only for his sake . . ."

I sat up. "For his sake what?"

Alan sat up, too. "Be nice to me!"

"Don't be a pain, Alan! Anyway, you're too old for me."

"That's a cruel blow! How old do you think I am? Twenty-eight?"

"I know you're eighteen."

"Definitely an older man. Probably a dirty old man. For Pete's sake, Jan, how old are you? Almost fifteen, aren't you? Three years is hardly a generation gap. I went out with a couple of your classmates."

"I know. I heard all about it."

"You shouldn't listen to gossip. It's an unladylike quality."

"Where did you get that—'unladylike'? You sound like something out of Louisa May Alcott. Who, today, is ladylike—whatever that means?"

"You are. I bet you're the only girl of your age and class who hasn't been kissed—plus a few other things."

I could feel the blood flow up into my cheeks. "That's a lot of nonsense."

"Ah, ha! So who's the lucky guy?"

I got up. "I think this conversation stinks, I really do." I went over to where Toby was nibbling the fresh sweet grass, took the reins and mounted. Then, without looking back at Alan, I rode off, through the pasture and back the way we came.

94

After a few minutes Alan came thundering up. "If you want to know what ladylike means, it means getting into a state because somebody merely said that you had probably never been kissed. It's the reverse of cool."

I shrugged. "Who wants to be cool?"

"Practically everybody. Want to race back to the barn?"

I would have loved to, but I was fairly sure that there were rabbit holes I couldn't see in the pasture and if Toby stepped into one he could break a leg. "Not here. I'll race you any day on a path."

Just before we got back to the barn, Alan put out a hand and stopped me. "There's something I want to say," he said.

"Okay. What is it?"

"It's that despite everything you've heard, and observed, I'm not solely motivated by the desire to win over somebody who's indifferent. I like you. I really like you."

"Okay," I said. I didn't know how to reply to that and it seemed mean to keep needling him. "Thanks."

Toby, anxious to get back to the barn, stamped. But Alan didn't let go. "It's Morris, isn't it?" he said. "Mr. Meow himself. He's the one you like."

The blood was back in my face. "Why should I tell you?" I said, fighting for time.

"No reason, but I know it is Mr. Four Eyes. Did you ever notice that his ears stick out?"

"Yes," I shot back angrily. "But he's more interesting to listen to and more fun than anyone I know." And I shook off Alan's hand and cantered Toby almost to the barn. After which, of course, I had to walk him until he was cool.

When Alan came back he didn't look at me. He just went into the stable and emerged again in the shortest possible time it could have taken him to unsaddle Mahatma. Still without looking at me, he walked over to the house where he was going to help Mrs. Smith with the rating questions.

One afternoon several days later I was mucking out one of the stalls when I heard Mrs. Smith's voice. "Judy, you simply can't take out Demarest. I told you, he's strained a tendon. You're going to have to ride one of the other horses for a while. Why don't you saddle Jasper? He could do with some exercise."

"Jasper's a klutz," Judy's voice was angry and edgey.

"Jasper's not a klutz. I don't have any klutzes in my stable."

"Well he's sure no Thoroughbred. He must have cost all of five hundred dollars."

"With all the riding you've done I'm surprised—in fact I'm shocked—that you judge a horse entirely by the price paid for him. Is that what you do with people?"

"Look, Aunt Jess, if you want to go all sentimental over cart horses like Jasper and Toby, then go ahead. I guess you have to be nice to people who help you make a living. But I don't have to pretend about what's a good horse."

I was standing there, getting hot with fury, when I heard Mrs. Smith's voice say, "Keep your voice down! Janet is mucking out here somewhere. If you could ride your highly bred Demarest as well as Janet rides Toby— who incidentally is a good horse—then I'd be surprised as well as pleased. And by the way, have you ever heard of a horse named John Henry? He was the biggest moneymaker in all Thoroughbred racing, but he was bought for a pittance—at least by racing standards."

"What do you mean I don't ride as well as Janet. I've won lots more prizes than she has."

"I mean that though you put on a nice perform-ance, it's all you. You don't care for your horse the way she does or work with him as well."

"Thanks a bunch!"

I heard Judy's booted feet stamp out of the barn, ringing on the stone.

"She doesn't know what the blazes she's talking about, Toby," I said, combing out his mane. "Pay absolutely no attention!"

Toby nickered and blew and rubbed his head up and down my shirt. Then he slyly edged his nose towards my pocket.

"Not until we come home, you thief," I said. "You can have a carrot then."

Almost half an hour later I was leading Toby out to the yard when I noticed that Border Boy's stall was empty. I had a feeling of surprise, but paid no attention to it as I got on Toby and headed towards the park.

It was a beautiful day. The trees were now leafy and full, and the air was filled with one of nature's great scents—the smell of wet grass. Long ago I'd named it the green smell, and the green smell followed me as I trotted and cantered along the trail, then followed a path up a hill and into the woods. It was a long ride, but Toby was fresh and full of beans. About an hour and a half later, we emerged from the woods to cross one of the fields when I pulled Toby up short. There, snipping grass, his rein dangling from his bit, was Border Boy.

Suddenly I knew why I had been bothered when I had seen Border Boy's stall empty. James Pendleton was supposed to be somewhere else on business for a couple of days. Who then . . . ? Judy, of course, I thought.

"Come on, Toby," I said and walked Toby slowly towards the big chestnut.

But Border Boy was in no mood to be approached. He started to move off in the opposite direction. It was then I noticed how lame he was. "My God! What happened to you?"

For a moment I sat there. Then I started calling. "Judy! Judy! Can you hear me?"

There was nothing—just silence.

"*Judy!*" I yelled as loud as I could, and felt Toby move suddenly beneath me. "It's okay, old boy," I said. "Just me, yelling."

I decided the first thing to do was to ride around the field to see if Judy was lying unconscious anywhere.

In the next ten or fifteen minutes, I crisscrossed the field as well as I could, keeping my eyes on the ground, concentrating on anything that could give me a clue. But aside from some rather deep hoof marks, I couldn't see anything. I tried calling Judy again, and there was still no reply. Where on earth was she? Probably walking back to the barn for help, I decided. Then I glanced at the path leading into the woods to see if I could find any hoof marks there. At least it might indicate where she and Border Boy had come from. But the path was smooth. She could, of course, have been riding among the trees, although it was an idiotic thing to have done, and it wouldn't be hard to imagine how Border Boy could have come by his lame foot if she'd tried to make him go through the undergrowth.

The only other possible explanation would be that she had come in the opposite direction from the wide avenue where I had galloped Toby so often. I touched Toby's side with my legs and we took off to the other side of the field. Even before I got to the path I could see that she had been there. Border Boy's hoofs were plain. Equally plain was a jumble of hoof marks plus some stirred-up dirt that would indicate where Border Boy had had his fall. And then suddenly I remembered James Pendleton saying that his horse was, strangely, more nervous in wide spaces than in closed paths lined by trees.

From where he had had his accident to where I first saw his hoof marks was more than the width of the field, so that he must have hobbled that distance on his lame foot. I stared at the mark and then back at Border Boy. Even if he let me approach him, what could I do? Nothing very much. But since I hadn't found Judy, I assumed she'd gone back for help.

Dismounting, I tied Toby's reins to a low branch of a tree so he could nibble some grass. Then I walked slowly towards Border Boy, watching him carefully as he watched me.

When I was about twenty feet from him, he gave a grunt and sheared off, limping and moving away from me.

I stood there for a moment, talking in my most soothing voice just loud enough for him to hear. But, of course, the voice to which he would respond best would be James's. And James wasn't there.

I made two more approaches. At the second he let me come up to him, still talking gently. I patted him on the neck and felt his skin, hot and wet to the touch. As easily as I could, I got his reins tied up in a knot on his shoulders so that he couldn't trip on them. Then gently, slowly, I stooped and touched his leg and felt a quiver go through him. The next thing I felt was a piercing pain in the middle of my back, and knew that Border Boy had bitten me. Just managing not to cry out, I got slowly to my feet and watched the big black horse move lamely off about twenty feet.

When I mounted Toby I felt the pain run down the middle of my back and down my arms. It was so painful I could hardly draw my breath. Well, I thought, I had to be the big hero. St. Joan of Arc to the rescue. With every trot, as Toby and I went across the field, I felt the pain jab into me. Cantering down the avenue was a little better, and I finally got across the dry stream bed and into the farm area. Mrs. Smith was grooming Aldebaran who was between crossties when I rode Toby in.

"Has Judy come back?" I asked.

"I have no idea. I haven't seen her. Why?"

Her words seemed to be coming from a distance, or through some kind of felt curtain. My whole back now felt on fire.

"What in heaven's name's the matter with your back?" Sally Lang, one of the barn girls said, coming up behind me. "You're bleeding like a stuck pig."

I had this clear knowledge: that there were two things that had to be done immediately. I had to get off Toby, and I had to tell Mrs. Smith about Border Boy. I decided to deliver the verbal message first. "Border Boy's in the big field in the park. He's lame."

Then I started on the second chore, dismounting. I leaned forward, there was a flash of pain. And that's all I remembered.

CHAPTER 12

"Ouch!" I said and opened my eyes. I was lying on a bench outside the tack room. The pain was awful. "What happened?"

"You fainted," Mrs. Smith said. "And small wonder, considering the bite on your back."

I started to sit up, and then caught my breath.

"Yes," Mrs. Smith said. "I'm afraid it will hurt for a while. Who is your family doctor?"

"Dr. J—" I looked at her. "Why?"

"Because I want to call him up right away and say you're on your way over to have him dress it and give you a tetanus shot."

"No," I said. "He'll tell Mother."

"I was planning to call your mother anyway."

"Please," I said. "Please don't, I'll go to a doctor, any doctor, but please don't tell Mother. That's all she needs to make me sell Toby. I told you how she is. With something like this she'll have all the excuse she needs to forbid me coming out here again. Please!"

Mrs. Smith paused, looking at me. Slowly, pulling myself up by the back of the bench where I was lying, I sat up. Then I put my feet on the ground. "I don't feel so bad," I said.

"Go in the house and take off your shirt. I want to look at that myself."

"What about Border Boy?"

"Sally went out to look at him. If you weren't so stubborn about not going to your doctor, I'd be out there myself right now." She hesitated. "I know James wasn't riding him, so I take it Judy was. I could shake her till her teeth rattle. She knows she's been forbidden to touch him. Border Boy's a highly nervous horse who needs experienced handling. Did you look for her?"

"Yes. I went all over the field and called. I couldn't find her."

"She could be anywhere. And she could have come back without being noticed. Practically everyone's somewhere else. Well, I'll have to worry about her, too. Now you get into the house. Go into the living room."

When I got to the living room I started trying to take off my shirt. I had no idea how many muscles were involved in doing such a simple thing, all of them feeling as though they were on fire. Undoing my bra was beyond me. But Mrs. Smith knocked and walked in just as I had come to that conclusion. She came over, gently unhooked me, then with her finger touched around the edges of the bite.

"It hurts, doesn't it?" she asked.

"Yes." I was determined not to make a thing of it.

"Well, Sally is given to exaggeration, and I think she exaggerated how badly you were bitten. There are tooth marks and in a couple of places your skin is broken, which is why it's bleeding. It's by no means the worst wound I've seen, but you're going to have a bruise the like of which you've never had before. And you must see a doctor. I don't absolutely insist that it be your family physician, although I think I must be getting soft-headed not to."

"Do you know anybody I could see?" I asked and then tried to hook my bra.

"Here! I'll do it! I'll call Dr. Carter. He's pro-horse, since he keeps his own here. And he's also one of the best doctors in town. I'm going out now to see Border Boy. I'll send Sally back, and she can drive you to his office."

Dr. Carter turned out to be a nice, slightly rumpled man with pictures of horses all over his office.

"Hm, yes," he said, when he saw my bruise. "Well, he could have given you a much worse bite, so he must like you."

"I'd sure hate to be bitten by him if he didn't."

"There now," he said when he'd given me a tetanus shot. "There's not much I can tell you to do, except put ice packs on it and beyond that, as much as you can, ignore it. But take baths instead of showers, because I want the dressing to stay on and also stay dry. You can come back next week and let me look at it."

"Look, could you please not send the bill home. Just tell me how much I owe you, and I'll bring the money next week." As he looked carefully at me, I said, "I don't want Mother to know. She doesn't like me to ride. In fact, she hates it, and this will just give her the excuse she wants to make me sell Toby. So let me pay you and that'll be that."

"Don't worry about it. And I won't tell your mother. How did it happen, by the way? Did your horse bite you?"

"Toby? Of course not. He'd never bite me. It was Border Boy, and he only did it because I was trying to look at his lame leg."

"Is that the big chestnut owned by James Pendleton?"

"Yes."

"And James was riding him? I thought he was out of town for the day."

"He is. It was Judy, because her horse, Demarest, is lame."

"I'll bet you he never gave her permission. She's a handful, that girl! How did it happen?"

So I filled him in on what had occurred.

"I sure hope the horse hasn't been badly hurt," he said severely. "That girl ought to be spanked."

I entirely agreed with him, but being my mother's daughter, I couldn't help noticing that he didn't even inquire as to what state she was in. He was right, I told myself. First things came first.

After I'd seen the doctor, Sally drove me back to town.

"I'll do your mucking out for you for the rest of the day," she said. "And I can get Toby settled."

But I did not want to go home at a peculiar time, because Mother might be there, or Cynthia. And if so, either or both could ask questions.

When I got back to the barn I went straight towards Border Boy's stall where I found Mrs. Smith and the vet. "How is he?" I asked.

"He's got a nail in his foot," Mrs. Smith said.

"Will he be all right?"

"With a lot of care and rest." She sounded grim.

The vet came out of the stall. "That's all I can do for the moment. I've given him a shot, along with his antibiotic, so he should be fairly quiet for a while. Don't look so glum, Jessica. It's nasty, but it could heal far quicker than you think." He glanced at me. "Is this the young lady who rode him?"

"No, it is not," Mrs. Smith said. She turned towards me. "How's the back?"

"Much better," I said.

"Well, you can go home now. I'll get Sally to put your bike in the back of her car and drive you. You could probably do with a little rest, too."

"I'd much rather go home at the usual time," I said and explained why.

"When would you ordinarily be going home?"

I glanced at my watch. "In about an hour."

"All right. But take it easy."

"Have you found Judy?" I asked.

"No. And we've been over every foot of any path leading into the field. And from the look of the avenue, just where it leads into the field, I'm pretty sure he threw her there. I can't imagine where she is. I'm expecting her father back at any moment. In fact," she said, moving so she could see the front drive, "here he is."

James Pendleton, dressed in a dark blue pin-striped suit, got out of the car, took his suitcase out of the back and started towards the house. But, probably alerted by the looks on our faces, he changed direction and came towards the barn, leaving his suitcase beside the front steps.

"Something tells me there's some kind of a crisis afoot. Does it involved Border Boy?"

"I'm afraid so, James," Mrs. Smith said. "And I can't find Judy."

He looked at the vet. "What?"

"A nail in his left foreleg, I'm sorry to say."

"Damnation!" James said. He went into the stall, talking quietly, and patted the big chestnut on the neck. "There, boy, whoa! Easy now, easy." He stooped and put his hand on the injured leg. I saw Border Boy shift and grunt, but he didn't seem inclined to take a bite out of James as he did out of me. After a moment or two, James rose, patted his horse again, and came out.

"Did Judy ride him?"

"Yes. I'm sorry, James. Demarest went lame. I suggested she take out Jasper—a suggestion she considered beneath her—and then I went off into the house to do something else. . . . About forty-five minutes later, Janet here found Border Boy in the big field at the end of the avenue riderless and limping around. She managed to get the reins tied up and then he bit her."

James, who had been looking grim, winced. "I'm sorry, Janet. He's bitten me once or twice. I can think of more pleasant experiences. Did he give you a bad bite?"

"Dr. Carter says it could have been worse."

"In the sense that he could have bitten off your arm, he's right. I love these medicos who are so philosophical about our injuries."

"Well," Mrs. Smith said, "he keeps a horse here so I thought he'd probably be as sympathetic as any, and wouldn't give her a lecture on the evils of riding as I'm afraid her mother might."

"That's right. She isn't the horse's best friend, is she? Well, I'll take you home and explain it."

"I don't want her to know anything about it," I said quickly.

"Janet, how on earth can you keep it from her? Every time you move you're going to feel it, and maybe show it. And if she even thinks of patting you on the back. . . ."

"Mother isn't given to patting me on the back, so it won't come up."

"You're surely not thinking of bicycling home yourself," Mrs. Smith said.

"No. It'd be great if Sally drove me. But then I could just say she was going my way."

"All right, if that's the way you want it. But if Mrs.

106

West comes breathing fire and blood at me, I hope you'll explain that I did want to tell her."

The next few days were a nightmare. Pain from the bruise kept me from sleeping much. The night after Border Boy bit me, I hardly slept at all, despite the ice pack that I tried to keep on most of the night. I had bought the pack itself from the drugstore on the way home, and sneaked downstairs twice during the night to fill it with ice, each time holding my breath for fear Mother or Cynthia would hear. Finally, I dozed off. It was luck I had set my alarm, because although I'm a natural early riser, I would have overslept. The hardest part was sitting up, and the next hardest part was getting out of bed. When I went downstairs for my bath, Cynthia, who was coming out of the bathroom, accidentally knocked into me. Before I could stop myself I gave a cry.

"What's the matter with you?" Cynthia asked. "Why the big fuss? I hardly touched you."

"Sorry," I said. "I guess I'm half asleep."

Cynthia peered at me. "From the way you look I'd say that's an understatement. Is Morris taking you onto the fast track these days?"

"Yeah," I said. "We covered all the disco joints."

"When?" she asked suspiciously.

"Last time we were out. Now will you let me get into the bathroom?"

She continued to stand in front of the bathroom door. "This is really interesting. You mean you've been going out with Mr. Four Eyes and not telling us? And all the time we thought you were babysitting, or doing something with your ridiculous quadruped."

"What's a quadruped?" I asked. The bruise was throbbing so painfully that I kept my front firmly towards Cynthia, sure that if she saw my back she could see it moving in and out.

"Horse, airhead!"

There's one thing about pain, I discovered. It concentrated the mind. Her insults rolled off me. "Move out of the way, Cynthia," I said. "Unless, of course, you don't mind my having an accident on Mother's new hall rug."

Reluctantly, Cynthia moved. "There's something fishy-looking about you today. If it's really the high life with Morris, then he must be on everything going. I don't think Mother would like that."

"Cynthia," Mother called from downstairs, "aren't you ready yet? And where's Janet? If you both want me to drive you to school you're going to have to get a move on."

I pushed open the door and closed it, locking it behind me. I started to lean against the door when I remembered not to.

A bath takes a lot longer than a shower, I discovered, so before I was dry, Mother was pounding on the door. "What's keeping you, Janet? I've never known you to be so late. Are you all right?"

"Fine!" I sang out cheerily. The bath had loosened me up a little, and I had swallowed two aspirin from the medicine cabinet. "I'll be ready in a jiff!"

"You're not going to have any time for breakfast. You've never done this before. Are you sure you're all right?"

I had a queer desire to say "No, I'm not. I feel lousy. And I'd like to stay home and do nothing." For a moment I almost succumbed. If it had been anything else—a flu bug, a sore throat, an upset stomach—then I could say so, and my mother would comfort me. But since it was a horse bite, then Mother was the enemy.

"Answer me, Janet!" Mother rapped on the door. "I know something's wrong. Now open the door and let me in!"

Hastily I crawled into my robe and then opened the door. "Nothing's wrong, Mom. I told you. I'm just fine. And I'll be right down."

Luckily, Mother had stepped back. I backed towards the stairs leading to my attic. "Couldn't be better," I burbled on, keeping my front towards her.

"Cynthia said you looked pale and drawn," she said slowly. "I'm bound to say you look rosy enough now. But I don't like your going to school without anything to eat."

"I eat too much, anyway. And I'll get some milk when I reach school. Must go!" and I hurtled up the steps two at a time, which would have been wonderful and effective if I hadn't fallen over the sash to my robe which I hadn't bothered to tie. Even falling on my front hurt, but I managed not to cry out.

Mother started up the stairs after me. "Are you okay, darling?" she said in such a loving voice that for a second I wanted to cry and wondered if she had mistaken me for Cynthia.

"Absolutely," I said, leaping up, Mother was halfway up the stairs behind me, so I ran the rest of the way and disappeared into my room, closing the door firmly. I'll be right down," I sang out.

I didn't at first hear her going down the stairs, so I slipped out of my robe and started putting on my bra, with the idea of getting my top covered before Mother decided to come up to see if I was, indeed, all right.

Pain shot up my back. I took a breath and waited. Then I heard Mother's feet going along the hall and down the main stairs. When I was sure she wasn't coming up, I abandoned the idea of a bra, put on my slip, sweater and then my skirt. In less than five minutes I was downstairs. Mother and Cynthia were waiting for me in the car. I slipped into the back seat. Once we were out in the street, Mother looked at me in the rearview mirror. "Cynthia's right. You do look pale."

"And if I didn't, Cynthia would probably tell you I was flushed and coming down with a fever."

"You're paranoid," Cynthia said. "Probably all that high living."

"What high living?" Mother asked.

"Ask Janet," Cynthia said.

"Well?" Mother's eyes in the mirror were back on me.

"There's a car coming," I said.

I saw Mother's head move and knew that she had looked hastily back at the road.

"I saw that. What high life?"

"No high life, Mom."

"Then what's all this about Morris taking you to discos?" Cynthia asked, and turned around from the front seat and looked at me.

"How's Alan these days?" I asked, knowing I was treading on a possible minefield. But I was tired of all the bitchery going one way.

This time Cynthia changed color. She went bright red. "You ought to know. You see him more than I do."

"What's that all about?" Mother's eyes were, once more, looking at me in the rearview mirror.

"Nothing, Mom," I said, as firmly as I could.

"Alan seems to prefer children," Cynthia said. "Apparently his new heartthrob is—guess who—none other than our own Janet! And it's horses that brought them together. Isn't that nice?"

"Here we are," I said with enormous relief as school loomed up on the right. Never before had I been so glad to see it. I had the door open before Mother had the car at the curb. "Thanks, Mom. See you tonight!" And I shot out of the car and ran across the schoolyard, my bruise throbbing with every step. I knew Mother was calling after me, but I pretended not to hear.

CHAPTER 13

Moving around the barn the next afternoon, mucking out the stalls and sprinkling fresh sawdust from a huge shovel wasn't the easiest thing in the world, but I managed it in only a slightly longer time than usual. Mrs. Smith came into the yard on Aldebaran just as I was finishing.

"How's the bruise?" she asked me as she swung herself out of the saddle.

"Oh fine," I said carelessly, forgetting that I didn't have to lie to her as I did at home.

"Wonderful!" She came up behind me and placed her hand on my back.

I gave a shriek and jumped away.

"Mustn't frighten the horses," she said with mild irony, and then, "I thought you were probably lying. Let's start all over again. How's the back?"

"Sore," I admitted, breathing in and out.

"I thought so. Terry!"

Terry put her head out of the feed room. "Yes, Mrs. Smith?"

"I want you to do Janet's mucking out, what's left of it, today."

"I've already done the stalls I was supposed to do, and I wanted to leave early to see an art exhibit."

"I'll pay you extra, of course," Mrs. Smith said. "Not that I'd want to get between you and your art studies."

I smothered a giggle.

"Well, all right," Terry muttered.

"And it isn't every day I'd call Joe Simpson an art exhibit," Mrs. Smith continued in a lower voice, so only I could hear it. Joe Simpson was Terry's boyfriend. He was all right if you overlooked his IQ, which must have towered at around a hundred. I giggled again.

"Isn't there anybody at your high school who's interested in horses?" Mrs. Smith went on to me. "I'd love to give Terry back to the art world. Her idea of taking care of horses is dim, a little better than nothing, but only just, and that's all I can say."

"All right," Terry said grudgingly, coming out of the feed room. She came over and took the big shovel from me. "You can do it for me some time."

I walked with Mrs. Smith and Aldebaran back to the grooming area. "How's Border Boy?" I asked.

"As well as can be expected for having suffered a nail in his foot. He'll be all right, in time. What worries me more is Judy and her relationship with her father."

"Where was she?" I asked. Somehow I knew she hadn't been lying injured somewhere.

"At a movie with your great friend, Alan. To do him justice, she didn't tell him what had happened, and he just assumed she had come home from riding in the usual way. When he brought her back, all hell broke loose. I don't think I've ever seen James so angry—not, of course, for her falling, but for taking Border Boy in the first place, when she wasn't experienced enough to ride him, and most of all for walking off and leaving him. If you hadn't come along, God knows how long he might have been there. If it hadn't been for that, I might have been able to stick up for her somewhat. After all, the hostility between her parents is not her fault, and she is very much its victim. But the most rudimentary sense of humanity and compassion should have prevented her from abandoning the wretched animal, which means, of course, she's a little short on those. I just don't understand people, Janet," she said, pulling hairs out of Aldebaran's brush. "Animals are helpless and powerless without us. We take them out of their natural state and domesticate them for our use and pleasure. And then people like Judy abandon them. I simply can't see how she can do it."

She applied the brush to Aldebaran's side. "I think you ought to go home now and back up on a sofa or bed with an ice pack. In the long run, you'll be better sooner."

"I'd rather take Toby out," I said.

"I'll exercise Toby for you. I think you ought to go home and rest."

"Like I said before, I don't want to go home at a queer time."

She looked up at me for a moment. "I take it you didn't tell your mother about your bruise."

"No," I said.

She sighed. "You're how old—fourteen?"

"Yes."

"Even at fourteen, if anything out of the way happens because of that bruise, your mother will have every right to call me on the carpet."

"Nothing's going to happen. And going out on Toby always cheers me up." I said after a minute, "Where's Judy now?"

"In her room, as far as I know. Or with Mia, probably enjoying mutual commiseration on how awful their parents are. In any case, she's been grounded.

Alan's been forbidden to take her out, and everybody warned that she's not to have either a car or a horse. I'm not sure that that's the right way to go about punishing her, but I didn't have much to say about it."

"Maybe if I went and talked to her—"

"No, don't! Unfortunately, while berating her, James sang your praises as being, by contrast, responsible. He's my brother and I love him, and I sympathize with how he feels, but he's certainly wrong this time in how he's handling his daughter. You're probably the last person she'd like to see—at least for the time being. What I'd like you to do," Mrs. Smith said, putting Aldebaran's tack away, "as I've said repeatedly, is go home."

"I'll just take Toby out for a bit first. I'll be slow and quiet, I promise."

It was a promise I meant to keep, and did so right up until we came to the broad avenue, where the temptation to gallop him was more than I could stand. "Come on, Toby," I said, patting his neck. "Let's have a little gallop. Right? No one need know."

Toby was fresh and full of himself, probably because he hadn't had quite as much exercise as he was used to. Whatever the reason, I found myself coming off in the middle of the path. There was no warning. I just fell off. And I fell on my back.

The pain was so great that, after an agonizing moment, I threw up. Somehow, I got my eyes open and looked around, terrified that because of my pigheadedness and stupidity I had caused Toby to be injured. But Toby was only a few feet away, nibbling grass at the edge of the path, his rein dangling. Like Border Boy, all he had to do was to take a wrong step, trip on the rein and break one of his legs. The horror of that prospect got me up on one knee. The ground waved and moved. What was left in my stomach heaved a little. I waited for a second or two for the spasm to pass. Then I got my foot under me and somehow stood up, hanging onto the branch of a tree. When I was steady on my feet I started slowly, very slowly, walking over to Toby. He stood there and let me approach him and, as I got within arms' reach, poked out his nose towards my pocket. One of my rules was: a treat only after riding. But there are exceptions to all rules, I told myself and Toby, as I felt his nose gently nuzzling my pocket.

Slowly, carefully, I mounted. Discretion was the better part of showing off, I decided, and trotted Toby soberly back to the barn. Twice during that ride it was all I could do not to pass out, and I wondered if as well as hitting my back, I had knocked my head. Unfortunately, along with other lapses, I had forgotten to put on my riding cap. But I didn't allow myself to entertain that thought. Instead, I concentrated on Toby and whether or not he was riding normally or if I had damaged him, too, in any way.

But Toby was his same wonderful self, and by logical steps this led me to think about Mother, who didn't even know him, didn't want to know him, and hated everything about him. How could you hate something you didn't know anything about, I wondered? The answer to that was easy: I hated the idea of calculus, even though I'd never had a word of it.

"But that's different," I said aloud, and then clutched the front of the saddle as a fit of dizziness seized me. "Whoa, Toby. Hold it."

I brought Toby to a stop and then sat there, trying to hold onto a balanced center as the dizziness came in another wave.

Somehow, stopping and starting, we got back. As I walked Toby into the barn I saw James Pendleton talking to Mrs. Smith. "There's something wrong—" I started to say, and then slid off Toby's back. Somebody—I think Mrs. Pendleton—caught me. The next thing I knew Mrs. Smith was gently shaking my shoulder and asking what happened.

I had one overwhelming concern. "Is Toby all right?" I said from where I was sitting on the bench. "Please see if he's all right."

"Toby is fine," James said. "Now tell us what happened."

"I fell," I said. Then, "I feel sick." And I was. "Sorry," I muttered.

"James, call Dr. Carter immediately. Tell him we're on the way to the hospital."

"No," I said. But nobody was listening.

I must have fainted, because when I came to I was in bed, but certainly not my own bed at home. I had a terrible headache, and it hurt to move. I lay there for a while trying to figure out where I might be and finally realized I was probably in a hospital, because there was a curtain along one side of my bed and a medicinal smell over everything.

"Where am I?" I said.

Two people suddenly materialized by my bed. After a moment I recognized them as James Pendleton and Mrs. Smith.

"You're in the hospital," Mrs. Smith said. "You hit your head."

"Toby?"

"He's fine," James said. He added, "The doctor said you will be, too."

"I forgot my cap."

"So we noticed." That was Mrs. Smith.

An overwhelming worry had worked itself to the front of my mind. "Does Mother know?"

"Of course. We couldn't not have told her. She's on her way now."

"She'll make me sell Toby," I said and started to cry.

"Hey, hey," the doctor said coming in. "What's all this about. You're going to be okay. It's only a minor concussion."

James reached down and took my hand, which was lying on the cover. "You may be wrong about your mother. But if you're not, I'll promise to buy Toby and hold him for you until you are free to ride."

"Thanks," I said, feeling like a fool. But no matter how much of a fool I felt, I couldn't stop crying. Everything—Mother's attitude towards Toby, the bruise on my back, Cynthia and her constant sniping from the side, the fact that I was never the favorite and that I'd never had a father to stick up for me, losing Toby—all rolled into one terrible lump. Worst of all was losing Toby. At that point the door opened, and Mother came in.

"What on earth . . . Janet?" she said.

Mrs. Smith looked up. "Mrs. West? I—"

"I knew something like this was going to happen. Well I can tell you right now, there's going to be no more of this—"

"No, no," I cried.

She came over to the bed. "I don't mean to make you feel worse, but when I got the call I had the scare of my life."

"Janet's going to be fine," the doctor said, moving towards Mother. "But I think what she needs right now is rest and lack of stress. So I suggest we all leave her and let her get some sleep."

"Yes," I said. "Please go."

"If she's supposed to rest and be alone, then what are these people doing here."

"They're going, too," the doctor added.

"I demand to stay with my daughter."

I had this sudden movie in my head of Toby being away somewhere where I could never find him again. "No, no," I yelled, sitting up in bed. "No!"

For a second, Mother and I looked at one another. She looked as though I had hit her across the face, and I was glad.

"Unless you want her to have serious damage," the doctor said, "You'll go, immediately."

I kept seeing this movie after they'd all gone. Despite what James had said, I saw Toby being led away to make pet food. It was like a commercial that kept going on and on. And it was all my fault. If I just hadn't gone out when Mrs. Smith told me not to, if I just hadn't forgotten my cap . . .

In a while the doctor came back. "Come on, now," he said, wiping my tears with a tissue. "I don't think your mother means half of what she says. She's one of those people who get angry when they're frightened. And you can't blame her for being scared. But the others are talking to her." He examined my head, then took my pulse. "Now I'm going to give you a shot and I want you to get some sleep. Everything's going to be all right."

"Not Toby," I wanted to say. But I was too tired.

When I woke up again I felt much better—in fact, almost normal. I looked around. There was no one in the room, and the other bed seemed empty.

I was thinking about sitting up, and maybe even getting out of bed, when the door opened and Mother came in.

"You're awake," she said. "How do you feel?"

"Lots better. Can I go home today?"

"Yes, I think so. Dr. Davis seemed to feel you were almost fully recovered. But he wants to see you while you're fully awake, before you get out of bed and start packing."

There was a silence between us. All I could think of was Toby and riding, and whether Mother had lowered the boom on both. The thought that she might have sent me back to feeling lousy again.

"What's the matter?" Mother said, coming over to the bed and sitting down.

There was no way I could think to handle it except straight out. "When can I go riding again?"

It was like watching something go from summer to winter. Mother's face went red and then white, familiar signs that she was angry. "I wondered how long it would take you—or your friends at that irresponsible stable—to ask that."

I knew the answer now. I closed my eyes.

"Listen to me, Janet. I don't want you to ride. Yes—" She said as I started to interrupt. "I know how you feel, but as I've said again and again, riding is a worthless, elitist and dangerous occupation, and I don't want to spend my life and money on your welfare, only to have you knock your brains out falling off a horse. They didn't even have the common gumption to make you wear your cap!"

"Mom! it wasn't their fault!"

"It was irresponsible of them not to keep an eye on you, especially after the accident I just learned you already had and which you didn't tell me about." She

120

looked at me. "How do you think I feel when you don't even tell me when you've been hurt."

"If I had you would have stopped me riding, just the way you're doing now." I wanted more than anything in the world to ask about Toby. But I didn't dare. I drew up my knees and put my face down.

"Yes," she said now. "I know how you feel about me. Wanting you not to hate me made me give in to you from the beginning, when you got that wretched horse against my wishes. Since then you've cared nothing about me, or your sister, or your home. Are you aware that you haven't even been to see Cynthia in the play?"

"What does it matter? She wouldn't come if I was riding in a show. Nor would you."

"You keep talking as though those two things were equal. They aren't."

I finally asked the question. "What's happened to Toby?"

"I neither know nor care. The only thing I'm absolutely certain about is you're not riding again. And the horse must be sold."

CHAPTER 14

For the next hour I begged and pleaded. Finally, I refused to go home.

"You have to come home, Janet. You know that."

"James said he'd buy Toby."

"I'm aware of that. But I'm not having you sneaking off and riding him when I'm at the office and don't know where you are."

"He's mine. You can't order him to be sold to somebody else."

"Yes, I can, Janet. I am your legal guardian."

"I hate you, I hate you, I hate you!"

Something in her face shifted. "I'm truly sorry about that. But it's preferable to having you brain damaged."

"I'll never leave my cap off again. I promise! Please Mom! Please don't make him be sold at an auction. Anybody could buy him—somebody who'd mistreat him, or sell him again for pet food, Please, Mom!"

There was a long silence. Then she said, "I'll drive a bargain with you, Janet. If you give me your word you won't ever go out there again and you will never ride again—at least as long as you're a minor—and if your . . . your friend, Mr. Pendleton, promises he will transport your horse elsewhere immediately, then I'll let him buy Toby and I'll put the money in your college trust fund. Agreed?"

"All right," I whispered.

When I got home, I was kept in bed for two more days, then at home for the rest of the week. Mother took the time off so I wouldn't be by myself. She never left me alone once. The phone rang several times. As long as I was in bed she would answer it downstairs. When I was up, if I was in the room, she would answer it before I could get to it. Sometimes she'd have a conversation with her secretary about something in the office. Twice she said, "May I call you back about that?" And then would leave the room, and I knew she was making a call from the extension in her bedroom. I was always sure it was about me or Toby. Twice, very quietly, I picked up the receiver when she was talking on another extension. Each time she said abruptly, "Just a minute. Janet, put down that receiver!" I obeyed only because I knew it was pointless not to.

I tried three times when she was in the kitchen or the bathroom to call the stable to make sure Toby was all right. But somehow, in some way, Mother knew and was at my side, putting her finger on the button before I could get through. Each time I lied, saying I was only calling one of the kids in class. "In that case," she would always say, "go ahead." And then I'd have to pretend I was too miffed to do it, because I couldn't even remember the telephone numbers of any of them.

I realized then that I didn't really know anyone. My whole life had been Toby, either babysitting or mucking out the stables to pay for him. The only person who was a friend, really, was Morris Blair. I thought about calling him, but what would I talk about?

That week was one of the strangest times of my life. It felt like I was in a long hall, not knowing where I was going, or what I hoped to find when I got there. I thought about Toby all the time, but after a while I saw that thinking about him made me so angry and filled with hatred for Mother that I'd feel sick. Then I'd make an effort to think about something else. When I didn't think about him, I thought about how soon I could get away from home, where I would go, and how I'd support myself.

Every night in bed I had wonderful, long fantasies: one was that the day I was eighteen I'd leave home. I would have saved money from babysitting and I'd simply get on a bus and go away as far as possible and would never see Mother or Cynthia again.

Another one that supplanted the first was that I would move out of the house and go to the stable and rent a room there. I'd buy Toby back from James and pay for his upkeep by coaching and mucking out. Eventually I'd win so many prizes that I'd be asked to join the United States Equestrian Team, and when I was interviewed in the papers I would describe in great detail just how Mother had mistreated me and how much I'd had to overcome. By that time Cynthia would have disgraced herself and the family in some really gross way.

Night after night I put myself to sleep with these fantasies.

Each day Cynthia came home from school as usual, chattering about her various activities, looking at me out of her long eyes to see if I had any reaction. Mother would say to me, "Isn't that interesting, Janet?" And I would say yes, because I was afraid not to.

Two or three times she tried to talk to me.

"Look," she said each time, "I know you hate me right now, but I'm doing this for your own good. You don't believe me—you don't want to believe me—but it's true. When I was going to the hospital to see you, all I could think about, or see in my mind, was Angela Blair and her crutches."

Finally, one night, I said, "You're lying. You're doing this because you hate me. You love Cynthia but you hate me. You always have."

I didn't know what Mother would say to that, and I didn't care. I sat there at the kitchen table, waiting to see what would happen.

Cynthia was in the kitchen, too. After I spoke, she drew in her breath. "That's an awful thing to say, Jan. And it's not true. It really isn't. I know what you think about me—"

I didn't even let her finish. "You were the one who said that Mother was being unfair to me. Remember? So don't pretend that it's not true." And I got up and left the room. When Mother called and said dinner was on, I told her I wasn't hungry. And I wasn't. But I would have stayed up there even if I was.

That night, the Sunday night before I went back to school, Cynthia came up the attic stairs and knocked on my door.

"Who is it?" I said, knowing it was Cynthia. Her footsteps sound different from Mother's.

"Cynthia," she said.

"What do you want?" I asked. I was lying on the bed staring at the ceiling. There was a stain on the ceiling from an old leak. It looked exactly like a horse.

The door opened and Cynthia came in.

"I didn't say you could come in," I said.

"I know. But I'm in. Jan—I know you're mad about your horse, but you're acting like Mother and I are in some cosmic plot against you."

"You are. You've been telling on me and stirring Mother up against me and taking shots at me for the past couple of years. I haven't said much because I was always afraid of what Mom would do to Toby. Well, now she's done it. I don't have to care any more. Get out of my room. When I'm eighteen, I'm going to leave home and I'm never coming back. I won't see either one of you again."

"You know, I think you're going nuts. You've never been like this before."

"I hadn't lost my best friend before."

"You can't be talking about that damn horse of yours!"

I leaned up on one elbow, found a book on my nighttable and threw it at Cynthia. She dodged and it didn't hit her. But she left the room.

The next morning I went to school. Between classes I found a pay phone and called the stable. I asked for Mrs. Smith but she was out trail riding, and so was James when I asked for him.

"Who is this?" the person—a boy—on the other end of the phone asked.

I opened my mouth to ask the same question. Then I thought if he found out who I was, he might tell somebody and it would get back to Mother. On an impulse I asked, "Is Mia there?"

"Well, she's supposed to be at school, but I'll ask."

I waited, filled with anxiety, because I didn't know when my quarter might run out and I had only one more, and also because somebody might come and want the phone. Finally Mia's voice said, "Hello?"

"Mia—it's Janet."

"Oh, Jan, I'm so sorry over what's happened. I don't share your feeling about horses, but I think your mother must be bonkers. She's worse than mine."

"Is Toby okay?"

"Sure. He's fine. Uncle James paid your mother for him, and he says he's ready to give him back to you as soon as you can have him."

What made me say it I don't know, but I heard the words coming out of my mouth. "Mia—would you ride him for me? He's used to a rider my age and weight, and I know James has his own horse."

"Damn it, Jan, you know how I feel about riding!"

"He won't throw you, I promise. He didn't throw me. I just fell off. If I'd listened to your mother I'd have gone home. I shouldn't have tried to ride him that day. But—" At that point the electronic voice that had been telling me I was out of time stopped and the phone went dead.

I started to dig out another quarter.

"You can't monopolize the phone," somebody said and then pushed me aside. "Give another guy a chance."

I spent the next two days worrying that somebody—the boy who answered the telephone, or Mia—would spread it around that I had called the stable. One of the conditions that Mother had laid down was that James would send Toby somewhere else. I got an awful pain in my heart when I thought of Toby going elsewhere, maybe to be ridden by someone who didn't feel about him the way I did, who wouldn't have a carrot when his nose came searching towards her, or his, pocket. It was such a terrible thought that I didn't do anything but think about it the whole day. We had a test in something, but all I did was draw horses all over the test papers. The teacher who handed them back thought the whole thing was very funny. And the F I got was funny, too.

The days went on like that. I didn't do any homework. I didn't care how I did on exams. From having almost all As and one or two Bs I was getting all Ds and one or two Fs.

After a few weeks of this my school counselor sent for me. "What's happening to you, Janet? From having been one of the best students, you're failing everything."

"Haven't you heard? I'm brain damaged. I fell off my horse. Ask Mother. She'll tell you all about it." And I left the room.

The one person I didn't want to talk to was Morris. I didn't quite know why. But it had something to do with the fact that he'd always been a friend, and I couldn't give him the same put down that I was giving everyone else. So I avoided seeing him when I could, which, given the fact that we went to the same school and had a lot of classes together, wasn't very practical. Whenever he'd try to catch up with me, or talk to me, I'd head off in another direction. One day, though, he cornered me.

"What's the matter with you?" he said. "I know your family's giving you a hard time. Everybody in school is talking about it. But I'm not. We used to be friends."

"I lost my best friend," I said. "And I don't have any others."

"The word is that your mother lowered the boom on your having a horse. I don't blame you for being mad, but what you're doing is crazy. It won't bring your horse back, and you're destroying your own chances."

"Chances for what?"

"Getting an education, for Pete's sake. Of having your own career."

"The only thing I've ever wanted to do is to have a horse. I worked for it and got Toby. . . ." But it wasn't safe to talk about Toby. "Get lost!" I said and walked away.

CHAPTER 15

The long war went on. I didn't think of it as a war. I thought of it as Mother's unfairness and Toby's banishment from my life.

At the end of the next week the principal sent for me. When I got there, he was standing beside the window of his office, looking out onto the playground, and beyond that, the trees of the town park.

"Well, Janet," he said, turning around, "have you declared war on the whole world?"

That was when I realized it was a war. "Yes," I said, pleased with the concept.

"But why declare war on your own future, on your schooling, which will mean, of course, on your chances for a decent college?"

"Because I don't care about that."

He came to his desk and sat down. "What is your horse's name?"

"Toby." As I spoke his name I felt the tears in my throat and back of my eyes.

"Tell me about him."

I didn't want to, because I knew I would cry. So I shook my head.

After a moment the principal said, "What color is he?"

"Gray," I managed to get out. "Sort of dappled. Kind of a dish face . . ."

The tears flowed then. I couldn't stop them. After a few minutes the principal cleared his throat and said, "I had a horse when I was a boy. He was named Rudolph, and I spent a lot of time fighting kids who said he was a rednosed reindeer. He was particularly partial to carrots."

I blew my nose. "So's Toby. When I come in, he pokes his nose at my pocket because I always carry a carrot there . . ."

Sometime later I ran out of steam. I'd been talking steadily about Toby for what seemed the entire morning but was actually about twenty minutes. "Sorry," I mumbled, blowing my nose again and wiping my cheeks. "I didn't mean to talk so much." And then I said, "Do you still ride?"

"No, I'm sorry to say. Somehow riding got crowded out. It's too bad, because I enjoyed it."

"Mother hates the whole idea."

"So I gather." He paused, then said, "Janet, what's going to happen about you and your Mother and about your schoolwork? I don't have to tell you that you're bright, one of the brightest in the school."

"Not as bright as Cynthia," I said.

"Cynthia doesn't carry the heavy outside load you do. Oh, yes," he said, "I'm aware of the babysitting and the stable work." He paused. "I take it you resent having to follow Cynthia's trail in school."

"Everybody always compared me to Cynthia. That is, until I got Toby. . . ."

"What do you want to do with your life?" he asked.

"I want to ride."

"Just that—ride?"

"Yes."

He looked at me a moment or two. "I can't promise anything, but I'll talk to your mother. You'd help your own cause a little if you started working."

"Mom can make me not ride. She can't make me work."

"Hmm," he said. Then he stunned me by saying, "The two of you are sure alike."

"No we're not. Cynthia's like Mom. I'm not."

"Yes you are. You forget, she and I grew up and went to school together. Cynthia looks like her. You act like her. Let either one of you get an idea in your head and it's war to the death. How do you think she put herself through law school when your father died, along with bringing up two children? Sheer stubbornness."

And then two days later, when I was at home by myself after school, the telephone rang. It was James Pendleton. "I know we all promised your mother that we wouldn't call or get in touch with you, but I feel I have to tell you . . . I'm sorry, Janet, but Toby has been badly hurt."

For a minute they were just words. Then I gave a cry. "How?"

"Well, different people have been exercising him. This morning Judy took him out, which makes me doubly sorry, since she's my daughter. She tried to jump him over a log. He tripped and fell onto a tree stump that had a long spike sticking up. The spike went into his chest."

"Is he . . . is he . . . ?" I couldn't bring myself to ask the terrible word.

"He's still alive. We called the vet, who came with the ambulance and took him to the clinic. The vet says he can treat him there for a few days, and if we give him full-time nursing at the barn for several weeks, he might pull through without damage. But that's expensive and time consuming. Janet, I know you love Toby, but he's not a Thoroughbred or a valuable horse. I hate to advise this, and it's not just the money—"

"Yes it is," I said, furious. "How much did the vet say it would be?"

James hesitated, then, "Two thousand dollars, and that is giving us extra consideration. Hospital care for horses is terribly expensive. But it's not just that. It's the time that somebody has to give. . . . Janet, if we let him go, then, when your mother is able to change her mind, I will buy you another—"

"*No!*" I cried. "No. I'm coming out there. Please, please don't let him die. Please James. I know he's your horse now, but I'll take care of him. I'll get the money somehow. I'm coming out now."

I didn't even wait to hear his answer. I just slammed down the phone and tore out of the house into the garage to my bicycle. Toby was at the clinic, of course, but I'd get somebody to drive me there from the barn. I don't even remember the bike ride, but it seemed to take forever. When I got there, James and Mrs. Smith were waiting for me.

"Park your bike, Janet," Mrs. Smith said. "We'll take you to the clinic."

Toby was in a tiled stall. A drain ran out of a wound in his chest. There were stitches there and the area around was bloody and matted. He looked so dejected. His head was hanging down, his eyes were half-closed and his ears were strangely floppy.

"Toby!" I cried. I went over and patted him and rubbed my hand up and down his nose and stroked his neck and kissed his forehead. "Toby, Toby," I said again.

He raised his head a little and made a vague gesture towards rubbing his face against my chest.

"That's the most life I've seen in him since we brought him here," the vet said.

I kept stroking and talking to him. Then I looked at the vet, "Does it hurt him?"

"Yes, of course. When we brought him back here we cleaned out the wound and got out some splinters." he paused. "I want you to know that it was Mrs. Smith and Mr. Pendleton who told us to bring him back. . . . Otherwise we probably would have destroyed him there."

I hugged his head harder than ever and looked at James and Mrs. Smith. "Thank you," I said. Then I asked the vet, "Can he get better?"

"Yes. But it'll take several weeks of very careful nursing after he leaves here. His wound has to be kept clean and drained, and a stable is not that antiseptic. And I don't think Mrs. Smith has someone who can do that full time."

"Yes, she does," I said. "I'll do it."

"Your school—" Mrs. Smith started.

"School is out in a couple days."

"What about your mother and her feelings about Toby?"

I looked up at her. "She can't drag me home. I'm almost as big as she is."

"No, but she can sue me," Mrs. Smith said. "You are her daughter and you are a minor. And I wouldn't be surprised if she could get a court order forcing me to throw you out. And Janet, I'm sorry. I'm not going to sacrifice my whole stable just to fight her in court. I don't think you could expect me to."

"No," I said. Then, "What about the two thousand dollars?"

There was a silence. At last James said "that's a fair amount of money, but it was Judy's fault, so I'll pay it."

"Thank you," I said again. "I'll try and pay you back."

He smiled. "No, I don't want to put that burden on you. I'm glad to do it."

I looked at the doctor. "Can he have a carrot?"

"By all means."

Toby's obvious pleasure over the carrot encouraged me. "When will he go back to the barn?"

"On Thursday."

That was four days away. School would be over. I had a lot of work and planning and pleading in front of me. But I was quite determined, no matter what anybody said, I was going to look after Toby.

"Can I stay with him now for a while?" I asked.

"Yes, but don't get him excited. I've given him a sedative. Just stroke him and talk to him a little if you want to."

Sometime later Mrs. Smith came by the stall. "We're going back now."

"All right."

I gave Toby another stroking and a kiss and promised I would see him the moment he got back to the barn.

When we reached the stable Mrs. Smith said, "I'm afraid I have to mean what I said, Janet. If you want to stay here during Toby's recuperation, that's fine with me. We've plenty of room and it will free everybody else for the work of the barn. But I can't do this with the fear that your mother might slap a court order on me at any time. I don't have the money to fight and I can't take any away from the stable itself. Do you understand why I say this?"

"Yes. It'll be all right. I promise. I'll call the clinic every day to see how Toby is. Will you let me know as soon as he comes home?"

She nodded. "I will." Then, as I got out of the car, she said, "Good luck."

James, who was seated in the back seat, smiled and repeated it. "Good luck."

CHAPTER 16

It was seven-thirty when I got home. Mother was just finishing dinner.

"Where have you been, Janet?" she asked. She had just taken a chicken out of the oven and was busy arranging vegetables around it.

I took a deep breath. "Out at the veterinary clinic. Mom, Toby was almost killed in an accident." The moment I said that, I knew I fed into her worst fears: horses make accidents. Quickly I said, "Nobody was hurt. Just Toby. He fell against the spike of an old stump. It went through his chest and . . ." I didn't want to cry now. I had spent the whole ride home planning my course of action, looking at it from every angle, so that I could get to nurse Toby, no matter what. I took a deep breath and said, "The vet cleaned out the wound and sewed it up, but he still has a drain in it, and when he gets back to the barn Thursday, he's going to have to have somebody to look after him all the time."

Mother didn't say anything for a moment, then, "Your principal and some of your teachers have been calling. Up to a few weeks ago you got mostly As. Since then you seemed to have gone on strike."

"Yes. But Mom, you knew I was."

"I kept hoping you'd see what a dumb thing that

was to do. You're ruining your whole life just to get back at me." She brought a big serving spoon down on the table with a clatter, splattering chicken juice. "What I can't understand is why! Tom Slater, the principal, had the nerve to say you were like me. When I was your age, all I wanted to do was to do well. All you want to do is—"

"Toby's my best friend."

"You can't have a horse as your best friend. That's ridiculous!"

"No it is not ridiculous!" I was shouting. "Toby never compares me to Cynthia. He doesn't care whether I make friends or not. He's my friend. He likes me. He thinks I'm great. The vet said when I talked to Toby this afternoon, he perked up more than he had with anybody else. I'm important to him."

"You're important to me.

"No I'm not. You just want a successful daughter."

"That's not true, Janet! That's simply not true."

"Yes it is. You don't care what I like."

Cynthia walked in. "Janet—"

"And you be quiet!" I yelled at her.

I turned back to Mother. "You're going to get your way in the end, so why don't you just listen to me. I want to be with Toby for the next six weeks. I'll study when I'm not nursing him. I'll ask the principal if I can take the exams again. I bet he'll let me, if you don't stop him. I'll get good grades, Mom. I'll do what you want. And when Toby is well I'll let James sell him to somebody who'll care for him." I stopped and took another breath. "If you don't let me, if you try and force me back here, I'll stay on strike. I won't crack a book, this summer or next year. I'll run away as soon as I can. If I get into drugs, then it'll be your fault."

"Are you threatening me?"

"Why not? You've been threatening me ever since I got Toby."

The interview with Mr. Slater was much easier. "Sure, Janet, if you study while you're out there nursing Toby, you can take the final tests again during summer school." He paused. "What does your mother say?"

"I told her if she didn't let me do this, I'd never crack another book and I'd take the first chance to run away from home."

"So the war is still on."

"I didn't start it."

"I don't suppose you thought of appealing to her."

"I've appealed to her and been nice and tried to do what she wanted ever since I got Toby. It didn't do any good."

"As I said. You're very alike."

Right after I'd seen the principal, I took a totebag filled with a few pieces of underwear and a lot of books, tied it all on my bicycle and went out to the barn. I told Mrs. Smith what had happened.

She sighed. "I take it your mother didn't actually say it was all right for you to be here."

"No. But she doesn't want me to drop out of school either, which I'll do. I'll become a drug addict and maybe a prostitute." A couple of weeks back there'd been a TV movie about a fourteen-year-old girl who ran away from a cruel parent and took to drugs and the streets. I cried all the way through it.

"Don't be absurd, Janet, and don't dramatize yourself like that. You know I'm sympathetic to your feeling for Toby. But I'm sympathetic to your mother, too. Remember, I'm trying to cope with Mia. You and she seem to think we—your mother and I—should do exactly what you want, no questions asked, whether we think it's good for you or not."

I was stunned. "I thought you were a friend."

"I am. But I'm also a mother. All right. You can have the room across the hall from Mia's. She's away in camp right now. And I hope when you're not nursing Toby and helping out in the barn, you'll study."

After that Mrs. Smith and I didn't talk as much as we used to, but it was all right, because I was with Toby.

He came back a day early from the clinic. He looked thin and didn't have much vitality. I cleaned his wound out with some stuff that the vet sent with him. I washed off the blood and the stuck hair and gave him daily shots of penicillin after the vet's aide had shown me how. When Toby snorted and pranced, the aide said, "He doesn't like it. No horse does, any more than we do."

But when I did it by myself the following day, Toby's skin just quivered, and he didn't make any more fuss.

"It looks like it's healing," I said one day to Betsy.

She came over and looked. She didn't say anything, so I finally asked, "Isn't that what it's supposed to do?"

"If it's healing from the inside out, yes. But sometimes wounds like that close at the top and stay infected inside."

"I'm sure this is healing properly."

"It seems okay. Do you want Mrs. Smith to check on it?"

I hesitated. Then I thought of Mrs. Smith's new coolness towards me. I shook my head. "No, thanks. I can manage."

But Toby didn't seem to be getting better. He didn't eat as much as he should, and even his interest in carrots flagged.

I went on cleaning the wound, using the alcohol-based liquid and the salve. When I wasn't doing that, I helped around the barn with mucking out and polishing the tack and trying to be useful.

I kept thinking Mrs. Smith would get to be her friendly self again, but she didn't. James Pendleton had gone back to the West Coast for a while, and Judy had gone to see her mother in London.

When I wasn't looking after Toby's injury or working in the barn, I studied. Usually I studied sitting on the straw in Toby's stall with my back to the partition. He seemed to like to have me there, and between books I'd talk to him. He'd whiffle or nicker and shove his face at me, but I couldn't help feeling that he wasn't recovering as fast as he should. Nobody seemed to think anything was wrong. Finally one day when Mrs. Smith was passing the stall, I went out and told her I was worried because Toby didn't seem to be getting better.

"Well, I can't check on him now, Janet. We're having a crisis with another horse who's just bolted out of the barn. Is his wound opening up?"

"No. I just don't think—"

She glanced in at him. "He looks all right to me, Janet. These things take time. And I'm afraid we're all pretty busy."

"You'd think," I said to Toby that night, as I was sitting by his head crosslegged with a book on my lap, "you'd think she'd pay a little more attention. She might as well be Mom."

Funny, I thought, running my hand up and down his jawline, it was the first time I'd consciously thought of Mother. Even funnier was the pang that went through me. I'd never before missed her, because we'd never been apart. But then the memory of our bargain washed over me. How could I even think of missing her when, because of her attitude about my riding, I'd have to sell Toby as soon as he was well?

"I don't miss her," I said out loud.

"Miss who?" Mrs. Smith's voice said from across the barn.

"Mom," I said.

"Why don't you give her a call?"

For a second I was going to run out and do it. I could almost see the telephone, and I could almost see our house and my bedroom and Cynthia, eating some yoghurt as she sat at the kitchen table, studying. It was so real it was weird. Then I remembered again how they both felt about Toby, and that Toby the Splendid was for me the most important person in the world.

"I said," Mrs. Smith said, appearing in the doorway of the stall, "why don't you give her a call?"

"Because she hates Toby and I know what she'd say."

"I see," Mrs. Smith said and walked away.

Then one morning when I came to the barn I knew Toby was ill, his head was hanging down. He didn't even move his head when I waved a carrot. I ran to get Mrs. Smith. She took one look at him and called the vet.

"This thing's closed wrong," he said. "It's healed over the top. You shouldn't have let that happen. Now I'm going to have to open it up again."

"Will he—will he be all right?" I asked.

"I hope so. But you're going to have to do a better job of cleaning off the scab and making sure the healing is done inside."

An awful lot of pus came out of poor Toby's wound, and when it was finally over, he looked miserable.

I felt terrible and very guilty because I hadn't taken good care of him. I stroked his neck and whispered to him and gave him a kiss. He made a vague gesture as though he would rub his face against me. But he couldn't quite make it.

Humbly I went to Mrs. Smith and Betsy. "Please show me how to do it properly," I said.

After that one of them came over once or twice a day to check on the wound. In another several days, it started to look better, and then Toby really began to recover.

At night I would sit there beside him and study my math and science and social studies and sometimes would read to him. He seemed to like French best and once or twice whiffled with pleasure.

A week later I led him around the ring outside and of his own accord he started to trot. His coat improved, and he began eating again and foraging in my pockets for carrots. A few days after that I asked Mrs. Smith if I should try to ride him. She nodded and said to start slowly and work up. So I walked him the first day and then trotted a little and by the end of the next week a slow canter. He responded with enthusiasm, and I had to restrain him from going into a gallop.

It would have been pure joy, except for the knowledge that I had bought this time with Toby by promising to let him be sold. I couldn't even bear to think about it. Normally, I would have talked to Mrs. Smith, but, except where questions of his recovery were concerned, she maintained her coolness.

One day I was busy brushing Toby when a voice said "Hi!"

I turned in surprise. There stood Morris, only I hardly recognized him. Even in those few weeks he had grown. His legs seemed unusually long. And then I noticed he had on boots.

"Have you come to ride?" I asked.

"I decided I might give it a whirl."

"I thought you were working for the summer."

"Not on Saturday, for Pete's sake. Is this the great Toby."

He came over and laid his hand on Toby's back. "What did he do, run into a spike?"

"How did you know?"

"Ma. She got the details from your ma. As a matter of fact, she sort of encouraged me to come out and start riding again. She's even paying for it."

"Why?"

"I think as a sort of example to your mother. Apparently your mother broke down one day in the office and they had a long heart to heart. Your mother asked Ma if she didn't regret ever riding, considering her lameness. And Ma said no, any more than she wouldn't get on a plane just because a friend she liked a lot was killed in an air accident. I mean, I guess she tried to get over the idea that you can't spend your life in a security bubble. Anyway, it was after that she said I ought to come out here and see if I liked to ride, and incidentally see you."

Morris rode better than I thought he would, although he had a little trouble with the English saddle and the Eastern style. But he soon picked it up and rented a horse for himself. After that, he came out two or three times a week. He also helped me with my math and science.

If it weren't for the promise I'd made Mother it would have been a great time. Toby was now almost well. And Morris and I would ride out a lot together in between my barn chores and studying.

One day Mrs. Smith got a letter from the school in Virginia she wanted Mia to go to saying that she had done well in the exams and was accepted. Two days after that, she got a letter from the school near New York saying the same. She was pleased and came and told me about them.

"Mia and I have you to thank," she said. "I'm really grateful, Janet."

She was being nicer to me than she had been the whole time I'd been there.

"Where will she go?" I asked.

"I've decided to leave that to her," Mrs. Smith said. "I guess I have to start letting her do her own deciding."

One morning I looked at the calendar in the stable and realized I had been out there five weeks. Then I found myself wondering what Mother and Cynthia were doing. There had been some talk about our going to western Canada for vacation. There'd been other talk about Cynthia going to England with a couple of friends from school and one of the teachers. I had deliberately shut my ears and shown no interest.

And then suddenly I wondered if Mother had become a partner.

I also wondered why she hadn't got in touch with me. For all she knew I could have died in some hideous accident. . . .

"Like I said," I told Toby one day. "She doesn't care."

When Morris came next time I said, "Do you know if Mom became a partner."

"Yeah, she did. There was a celebration at one of

the expensive restaurants that night. Ma and I were invited. Your mother and Cynthia were there with the other partners being toasted and so on."

I had a queer pang. Nobody had invited me.

A week later I got on my bike and went into the school and for two days sat for all the tests that I'd either ignored or screwed up. "I hope I do okay," I said to the teacher who gave them to me.

"I hope you do, too. How's your horse—what's his name?"

"Toby. He's much better. In fact, he's fine."

Fine enough, I thought resentfully, for me to fulfill my promise to hand him back to James and say that he could sell him to somebody who'd care for him.

I kept waiting for Mother to get in touch with me and to tell me that I now had to perform my part of the bargain.

And then one day, without thinking about it ahead of time, I caught a ride into the town and showed up at Mother's office.

Mrs. Blair was sitting at a desk outside. Her crutches were leaning up against the bookcase behind her.

"Hello," I said.

She turned. "Why Janet, how nice to see you! How's Toby?"

"He's fine. He's okay now. Is Mom in?"

"Yes. Let me see if she's with anybody?"

I sat down while Mrs. Blair pressed a button and talked on the phone. When she put down the phone, the door to Mother's office opened and she stood there.

"Hello, Janet," she said. "How's Toby?"

"He's fine." I was surprised to find that I wished people would stop asking about him and start asking about me.

Mother smiled. "And how are you. You look very well."

"Yes."

There was a silence.

"Did you want to see me about something?" Mother said, exactly as though I were a client.

I took a breath. "I took the make-up exams."

"I know. Tom Slater called and told me. Early reports are that you did well."

"That's good." I paused. Then, "We had a bargain. I said I'd let James sell Toby when I was sure he was okay and if it was somebody who would care for him." That part was still hard for me to say. "Well, he's okay."

"Do you want to sell him?"

"Of course not."

"All right. You don't have to. Between Tom Slater and Angela here and Mrs. Smith, I've seen the light. I'm sorry you and Toby had to suffer so much for my mule-headedness. But, finally, the penny dropped. You want Toby, you can keep him. You don't have to become a drug addict or a prostitute."

I could feel the blood pouring up into my face and as vaguely aware of heads popping out of doorways. "I suppose that was pretty silly."

"Let's say extreme."

"Well Mrs. Smith doesn't like me any more."

"Yes she does. But she's a mother herself. And I think she wanted to be sure she didn't appear to set up her maternal role in competition."

All this time Mother was leaning against the doorway. She looked well.

"By the way," I said. "Congratulations on being a partner."

"Thank you."

"You never even called to see how I was."

"Yes I did. Mrs. Smith and I had frequent conversations. I was assured that you were in good health, working hard and apparently happy."

"And you knew you weren't going to make me sell Toby. You could have called and told me."

"If you had called me, or Cynthia, to see how we were, I would have been glad to tell you."

Finally, pushed by an overwhelming need, I said, "I missed you."

I saw her eyes fill with tears. "For real?"

"For real. Can I come home?"

"Oh Janet," Mother said as she hugged me. "I thought you'd never ask." She was crying, but she was also laughing.

About the Author

Isabelle Holland sold her first story at the age of twelve to an English comic book. She has been writing ever since—all kinds of books for children and adults: mysteries, love stories, family stories, and animal stories.

The daughter of an American Foreign Service officer, Isabelle Holland lived with her family in Basel, Switzerland; Guatamala City; and Liverpool, England. She came to the United States to complete her studies at Tulane University in New Orleans, and she has lived since then in New York City with her typewriter and her cats and stacks and shelves of books.